THE DARKLY STEWART MYSTERIES

Light and Darkly

DG Wood

www.darklystewart.com

ISBN: 154135821X
ISBN 13: 9781541358218

"I love storytelling, and I love police work, and so I found this story to be perfect. I am grateful that in my almost 20 years in law enforcement as a Philadelphia PD Detective, I have not had any such investigation that Darkly had in this story. I applaud DG Wood for somehow making me actually want to become a werewolf. In the world that DG Wood created, it's sexy to be a werewolf. It's exhilarating, there is so much life, so much inner power and peace. There was much talk about it being a curse to be a werewolf. But in the world Wood created, I found it to be a curse to be human. As a Detective, I wish I had the instincts Darkly had, I wish I could smell death."

—Domenic O'Neill, Philadelphia PD.

"For all of you who have had strange experiences in small towns, reading The Darkly Stewart Mysteries will either make you want to go back and visit, or hope you never run out of gas on the highway.... Either way, you won't be able to put it down!"

—Todd Witham, Director/Screenwriter.

"I have a crush on Darkly Stewart. She's a strong heroine created by the unique mind of author D.G. Wood in an exciting and original, fast-paced story that I couldn't put down. Mystery/Adventure lovers, I think you won't be able to either!"

—Lieutenant Commander Daniel McShane, U.S. Navy

ACKNOWLEDGMENTS

I wish to thank Lorraine Berglund of Carousel B Productions for her unwavering support as my producing partner for the last several years. It has been among the most productive times of my life. Much gratitude goes to Graham Ludlow, who saw clearly that the potential of Darkly must not be limited to print, but that it must also find a home in the form of television adaptation. Without Jennifer Goldhar of The Characters Talent Agency, who has been my agent and friend since the turn of the Millennium, I would not have access to world-class talent to populate the world of Darkly Stewart. And to my brilliant agent in the UK, Frances Phillips, I appreciate your guidance in sending me off on a North American adventure almost twenty years ago now. We're all in for one howl of an adventure.

To the two cities my wife and I love so dearly, London and Los Angeles, I ask that you pardon small liberties taken with walls, trails, and toilets for the sake of story.

To my wife, who waits patiently for a return to the romance that is life in London, I say it is coming. All the long hours in development and the writing room are spent to that end.

To my colleagues at The Camera House, I say that to come to Hollywood and find a professional home with all of you in the industry I love, is the stuff less fortunate others dream about. I do not take it for granted.

And special thanks to all those who took the time to sing Darkly's praises!

For Audrey, Maria, Fiona, Blake, and Simon.
Together, you define friendship…

…and for Jamie and Tanja. Welcome to the club.

"The wolf also shall dwell with the lamb…"

— Isaiah 11:6

PROLOGUE

Nebuchadnezzar clawed his way through the red dirt with hands he had not used in more years than he could recall. This was a man dragging himself back from the wilderness. A man reborn. He reached the stream's edge and looked down at the moving reflection, startling himself. Nebuchadnezzar vomited. The haze in his mind was clearing, but his natural visage was alien and unnatural to behold.

The young wolves had followed him to the stream, whimpering from a lack of comprehension at the transformation that was taking place. Their fear surpassed their curiosity when the Angel of the Lord descended upon Nebuchadnezzar, and the wolves retreated into the cover of brush.

The Angel's feet slipped through the water, and ripples washed over Nebuchadnezzar. He waited for death.

But, the Angel of the Lord lifted Nebuchadnezzar to his feet and said, "You are a beast no more. Stand as a man stands."

Nebuchadnezzar's naked body shook from the cold. So, the Angel commanded him to sit and called the wolves to the man's side. They came, unafraid, for the Angel of the Lord wished them to be so. The beasts wrapped themselves around the man and warmed him.

"You are redeemed, Nebuchadnezzar," proclaimed the Angel. "Let your children of the wilderness be a constant reminder to you and your descendants of past sins."

Then, the Angel of the Lord became like the water he stood in, maintaining his shape for a split second, before collapsing into the stream.

—∗—

Eluned crossed the Royal Mile and disappeared once again down a snicket that eventually deposited the queen onto an Edinburgh road much less traveled by the citizens of Scotland's fairest city.

Eluned was Welsh herself, but had married a Scots doctor and embraced her husband's native city. Sadly, he lost his life in the great Darien scheme, succumbing to the disease he had been hired to treat. It had been the greatest feat of business ever devised by the mind of men. Scotland set up a colony, whose chief purpose was to transport the goods from one ship across the narrow isthmus that separates North and South America and load them onto a ship on the other side, so that the goods may complete their journey to Asia. Ship captains were saved the perilous journey around Cape Horn, and months were shaved off delivery times. A masterful scheme, if not for unforgiving fate. The tiny mosquito wiped out the colony.

Now, with Scotland's coffers emptied by the failed scheme, the union with England could not be stopped. It's 1700 A.D., and Eluned had just been proclaimed Queen of Wolves. She saw her duty clearly. Great changes were on the horizon. Hiding the true nature of her people was a daunting task during the ever forward march of progress. An exodus of wolves from the British Isles, and a relocation to the vast, virgin forests of the Americas, would be her legacy. She would travel much farther north than her husband ever did.

Since the time of Boudicca, the descendants of Nebuchadnezzar had chosen a woman to determine the way forward every hundred years. The alphas of a pack must always be men. Eluned knew it would be centuries, if ever, that a woman would hold such a rank. There was more chance of women being admitted to the priesthood. But, for the next hundred years, even after her passing, the werewolves of Europe would live their lives per the tenets she laid down during her reign. At the turning of the next century, a new queen would be chosen, and all Eluned's work would be upheld or undone.

The queen was forty-six. She may not live but another decade or two. It did not matter. Her commands would be obeyed until 1800 A.D. This awesome responsibility was at the forefront of her thoughts when she pushed open the door to The Hanging Tree pub.

Eluned nodded at the landlord, who stood watch over two chronic drunks snoozing at a table in the corner of the small room. She walked past the bar and through another door that opened onto a circular stairwell. The steps, several hundred of them, led deep underground. The flash of light at the top of the well gave way to flickers of light below, and Eluned walked forward on flat ground, moving through a tunnel lined with torches. The walls were damp and carved with the figures of wolves. Wolves hunting, wolves mating, wolves transforming back into the human.

Twenty-five yards on, the tunnel opened into a natural cavern that was two feet lower than the lip of the tunnel. The cavern was illuminated with enough torches to make the space almost as bright as day. The floor of the cavern was covered in tapestries. On the walls, where the tapestries should have been hanging, were specks of starlight imbedded in the rock. With but one torch lit, the cavern must have resembled the galaxy in the night sky.

Eluned stood above the room and smiled kindly at the men below, her most important subjects, who would implement her mandate. The irony of undertaking a mission similar to the one that got her husband killed was not lost on the queen. One of the men, Colonel David Black, placed wooden steps below the wolf queen's position and held out his hand to help her down.

The colonel was the linchpin of Eluned's designs. He had served in the English Army in the New World. He had successfully navigated the politics of tribal alliances in the colonies. Rumor had it that Colonel Black had married an Indian maid in the ceremony common to the savages. In England, his legal marriage was to the youngest daughter of a peer of the realm. It was a step up the establishment ladder that had handed him his present commission. No wolf had achieved such a seamless assimilation before. But it must now come to an end. With his wife converted, and his children born wolves, it was only a matter of time before sheer numbers resulted in eventual discovery, persecution, and massacre.

So it was now that Black, representing the English packs, and those representing the packs of Wales, Scotland, Ireland and France stood before her, ready to swear absolute allegiance to her. There were wolves in the farthest reaches of Europe and beyond. Those of the steppes of Asia had been hunted to virtual annihilation by the Mongol horde. They fled west to the vast, tangled forests of eastern Europe. There, the wolves of Romania, the Ottoman Empire, the German-speaking duchies, and the Danube lands eked out an unconstructed, lawless existence. It was several queens before Eluned who had consigned them to eventual extinction.

The men accepted the duty that lay before them. The ships were bought and sailors seduced to man those vessels of exodus. They would be the first new wolves for a new life in a new world. A place where there would eventually be no need for a queen. By the end of the century, North America would belong to the wolves, and Great Britain would be a memory of only the very old.

Of course, the best laid plans can and do perish in conflagrations fueled by naivete and set aflame by intolerance and fear. It was Colonel Black who would forge a secret confederation between the wolves and the British Army, which would serve the United Kingdom well, as it pushed ever westward and northward against the frontier and the French. That alliance was on the way out, when the wolves were betrayed after victory on the Plains of Abraham.

With General Wolfe, protector of the wolves, dead, younger men who saw no future need for a deal with such devils, ended the confederacy in brutal and bloody fashion. And so, as the followers of Boudicca fled west to the mountains of Wales almost two millennia before, after their defeat at the hands of Roman legions, so too did the wolves of the New World fly further west and north for the impenetrable barrier of the boreal forest.

It had been a shortsighted decision on the part of the British Army. For, a generation beyond Wolfe, they would needlessly lose the colonies to a rabble of farmers with antiquated weapons. If the old alliance with wolves had stood, the outcome of the American War of Independence may have looked very different.

There remained werewolves in Britain, roaming the moors and collected by the ruling class, who then put the wolves down with silver swords when they grew bored with the responsibility or the cost of replacing a field of slaughtered sheep.

In North America, as Eluned had foreseen, the idea of kingship was forgotten. Sheriff became the preferred term for Alpha Wolf. Frontier towns prospered and engaged in commerce with the outside world, with few incidents that couldn't be explained away with scapegoats from the dark and dangerous wilderness all around. The last Queen of Wolves was proclaimed in 1800. Her great commandment was to stick to one's own kind, not foreseeing the problems that would mean for the gene pool.

By the turn of the Millennium, with werewolves consigned to legend, and due to their self-imposed seclusion and embrace of puritanism, about to become myth, there were those who began to think that a queen may be just what the doctor ordered.

In the outside world, the institutions of democracy were showing wear and tear, and the gap between those who have and those who have not reached a point not seen for centuries. So, when the leaders of a small town descended from Eluned's colonists devised a plan to bring freedom to all, wolf and human, by making every human wolf...there was a woman among them who saw herself as Eluned's inheritor. If the plan was to succeed, the monarchy must be restored.

CHAPTER ONE

There was that taste. It reminded Darkly of pressing the tip of her tongue to a battery. The man appeared benign enough. Middle-aged, he wore an immaculate suit, and his expression revealed neither impatience nor a carefree nature. Darkly thought he looked like a CEO. Where was it that she read four percent of all CEOs were sociopaths?

Threat to society or not, this man standing in front of her at the post office had killed someone not that long ago. Was it a relative's suffering he brought to an end with an overdose of morphine? Or had this man recently fulfilled a taboo desire?

Darkly took a swig of the diet coke in her hand and shook it off. She looked down at the postcard of a vineyard in the Okanagan Valley and turned it over. The ends of her hair dripped due to the rain outside from which she had just escaped, and the ink was a little smudged as a result. But the message was still legible. *I'm safe. Don't worry. You'll see me again. Love, Darkly.*

Darkly thanked the trucker and climbed down from the cab. She'd found him in a diner on the outskirts of Vancouver, where she binged on complex carbs and proteins after flashing her RCMP badge and joining him in his booth. She had to get herself as far away as possible from any populated area, and Darkly didn't know when she would next eat a full meal. Would she feed when she turned? Would the need to hunt take hold instinctually?

At this moment, she listened to the eighteen-wheeler shift gears as it disappeared in a bend of the road up ahead. She was alone and as ready as she'd ever be.

Darkly estimated she was thirty miles from Wolf Woods. Maybe a little closer. The rain had not stopped pouring on the drive north, and Darkly pulled her water-proof hood tightly around her head as she left the road for the cover of the pine woods. Tonight, she would camp a few yards from the road, and then follow the highway for most of the next day. She knew how much ground an animal the size of a wolf could cover in a night. But she would not confront Wyatt until she knew the facts about herself. She would face those facts alone in the woods, and then she would kill the man responsible for the death of her family.

The night did not go as Darkly hoped. Or was that feared? She was as certain about how she felt on tapping into her true self as she was about confronting Wyatt. She would kill him. There was no doubt there. But, how? She didn't question that Buck had already dealt with the threat to his town. But, Wyatt is Buck's blood. He'd be banished again, to remain the constant and monitored threat. As a wolf, Darkly would be able to track him even easier than with her RCMP skills. And Buck would follow her, intent on rescuing her from nurturing a taste for murder.

There was something more. Darkly was beginning to understand why Wyatt was still alive. He was the bad example, the bogeyman, held up as the example to others of how it could all go terribly wrong – if they gave in to their baser instincts, if they adopted, too rashly, ideas of integrating with the outside world, if they chose to follow wolves other than Buck and Geraldine.

There wasn't even a moon on Darkly's first night. She knew it was there from the patch of bluish glow in the cloud bank above her tent, but she had imagined something different: Moonlight Sonata giving way to the heavy metal pulse of rushing blood. A pumping heart beating as fast as Darkly's feet – paws – carried her to her destiny.

Instead, Darkly awoke at dawn to the pitter-patter of drops of water falling off pine needles and landing on the tarpaulin strung above her tent. She ran her hands down her body, across her bare breasts, over her abdomen, and down to her panties. There they were. Panties. Darkly did not want her bra ripped to shreds, but also did not know if she could count on remembering her first time. So, she had left the panties on as a sign that would reveal outcome.

Failure. Had she indeed been cured? She looked down at the faded blue spider veins that leapt out from an empty place on her lower neck where a pendant once sat. Where it sat for her entire life up to that spontaneous decision forty-eight hours ago.

Darkly packed up her wet tent. She'd dry it out when the rain stopped. If the rain stopped.

The hike to Wolf Woods could best be described as soggy. Darkly was in good shape and motivated, to say the least, so she covered the ground in eight hours. What would she find at the end of her trek? A town flattened by a cyclone of fur and jaws? Was there even revenge to be taken? Had Buck brought a final end to the family feud with a localized flood of blood? Where did that leave Darkly? AWOL in about two and a half months. Then again, why wouldn't she return to duty?

Darkly approached the outskirts of Wolf Woods without inci-dent. She parted the sheep on a sloping pasture as she made her way down to the Moon River. Naturally skittish animals? Or did they sense her true nature? The last mile into town hugged the crescent-shaped bankside.

Darkly made her way straight to Sheriff Buck's office through a quiet town, an empty town. There wasn't a soul in sight. The door was unlocked. Again, no one. No sign of strife, none of the Robertson clan locked up. Darkly next visited the church. Maybe the town was giving thanks for Wyatt's defeat? She was greeted with immaculate silence.

Darkly decided to check in at the hotel. The front desk was unmanned, and the light switches did not illuminate anything. She tapped the bell. Lewis didn't poke his head out of whatever cupboard he spent most of his day in to tell her he'd really rather she found her way to another establishment.

While she was here, she might as well look in the rooms of the cast and crew from the horror film turned terrifying reality. Climbing the stairs, every squeak of the boards under threadbare carpet echoed throughout the building.

Darkly opened the door to her room and stepped inside. It was just as she left it. The bed was unmade, and an empty brown bottle from her impromptu picnic with Buck was jammed into the window frame to hold the window open. Just where she had put it. The paper-thin curtains rustled in a light wind. She looked out over the town for movement. Not even a tom cat revealed itself.

Darkly looked back at the bed. There were still a few hours left of daylight, and she should investigate this mystery further. She needed to find Buck and Gus. But she was tired after her hike, and she wasn't any use to herself exhausted. Darkly decided she would continue her search under cover of night. So, she shut the door and locked it, got into bed, slid her gun under her pillow and was asleep in a few minutes.

The creak of a rusty hinge jolted Darkly awake. The moon hung just outside the window and illuminated the room. Darkly reached under her pillow to grasp the handle of her gun and turned her head very slowly to look at the door. What she knew she had locked herself, was now open a crack. She could sense someone on the other side of the door. Watching her.

Darkly, her eyes never leaving the door, slid out of bed and held her gun pointed at the ground with both hands as she silently crossed the space between the bed and door. She slid her back against the wall next to the door frame and freed one hand to take her smart phone from her pocket and hit the flashlight app. Then, with one swift move, she shone the front of the phone through the crack in the door.

The screen's light reflected off the glint of a discarded gold key on the floor and then two eyes, which was followed by a loud gasp and the sound of feet escaping down the hallway.

Darkly swung the door open and leapt into action. She shone the light down the hallway, while pointing her gun at the darkness in front of her, ready to fire.

"Who's there?" Darkly commanded. "I'm an officer of the law."

Whoever it was, they were still on this floor with Darkly. She could hear them breathing. Darkly placed one foot carefully in front of the other, closing the distance between her and the end of the hallway.

Darkly lifted the light, scanning the hallway as she moved forward. The edge of the beam found pale, white flesh. It recoiled from the light with a whimper.

"I'm not going to hurt you."

Whoever cowered on the ground clearly did not believe Darkly, as he or she flew at Darkly, knocking her off her feet. Darkly fired, knocking the attacker back against the wall. The voice that screamed out in pain was clearly that of a woman.

Darkly picked herself up quickly and prepared herself to fire again. She grabbed her phone, that had been knocked to the ground, and shone it into the face of Marielle.

Darkly couldn't believe it. The corpse in the morgue turned to wolf was now sitting in front of her clasping a bleeding shoulder.

Marielle turned her face to the wall to escape Darkly's gaze. The back of her head looked like something out of a Frankenstein movie. It was a patchwork of over-stretched skin and clumps of hair.

"Is this Hell?" Marielle asked with a shaky voice.

CHAPTER TWO

Constable William Schilling left the structure of wood, bone and animal skins. He stood looking into the blinding sun, made all the more impossible to avoid by the snow that reflected its brilliance into every crease and pore of William's face. He lifted the caribou hide that sealed the family home from the elements.

Inside, there was a tableau of carnage. An Inuit mother and her two young children were wrapped in furs, each child placed gently under the arm of their mother by William. This was not how William had found them. The children's throats were cut. Cleanly. Unlike their mother. The mother had been stripped naked, and jagged cuts covered every inch of her body. More like rips in the skin. This was the third massacre he had encountered in less than a week. Each exactly the same. Committed while the man of the family was away hunting. The children killed quickly by their mother in order, he presumed, to save them from her own fate.

William looked at the knife in his hand. Its handle was fashioned from the tusk of a narwhal. The scene of the hunting expedition that killed the narwhal was carved into the shaft. He slid it into his belt and pulled the Inuit sun goggles hanging from a leather strap around his neck up over his eyes. The narrow slit in the center of the thin piece of wood limited William's scope of vision and protected him from snow blindness.

She had made them for him. The one who called him *ui*, which meant *husband* in the Inuit language. William was, in fact, married to a woman back in civilization. A good woman, whom he loved very much, in a way that a man like William loved a woman for no deeper reason than because she is his wife. There was no need to complicate matters with philosophy. But, William was more complicated than he imagined himself to be because he was two men living in two very different environments with two very different sets of needs. The man who stepped foot into the boreal forest or out onto the desolate tundra had desires that if not relieved would distract him from his job. Distraction in the north meant death.

In fact, his predecessor had encouraged such a liaison, and the predecessor before him. The British called them sleeping dictionaries. William's Inuit wife taught him the language and how to thrive in places that white men did not ordinarily survive.

His *nuliaq*, or wife, was young and wanted William often. When he was away from her and returned, they spent several days under the animal skins catching up.

William circled the encampment. He found what he was looking for. Paw prints. Wolf. Faint in the hard, compacted snow. But, the prints had a companion. An unwanted companion? The creature had followed hours, perhaps a couple of days, later, and they covered the paw prints in many places.

William looked back at the Inuit home for the last time. He had covered half a mile already. He looked down at the snow once again and the impossibly large footprint that created deep indentations in the frozen powder. William was not the only creature hunting the killer wolf. Perhaps it was the husband and father. Or not.

The sky was the color gray that meant snow. If he didn't hurry, William would lose the tracks. And that would be a hell of a birthday present. William Schilling was now thirty years old.

⚊⊣⊢⚊

The face was badly scarred, but Darkly recognized Marielle. She had looked into the girl's eyes, as Marielle had prepared to kill her not so many weeks previous. One tends not to forget such people. Darkly allowed herself a moment's distraction, as she contemplated her partner's final breath while holding him in her arms. Then a thought that truly shocked crossed her mind. The kid Marielle was fucking in the toilet stall…what had become of him? Is he still just a shy young man? Or something more now? Darkly would need to deal with that on another day.

"You're home," Darkly responded to Marielle in the softest, most reassuring voice she could summon.

"Then where is everyone?"

"I don't know."

Darkly reached out and gently touched Marielle's back. The girl flinched.

"What happened to you?"

Marielle buried her face in her arms, rolling herself up like a pill bug. Darkly, her compassion outweighing her revulsion, ran her fingers gently through the few wisps of hair left on Marielle's head.

"Shhh. You're safe. I promise."

Marielle no longer flinched. She merely rocked her body back and forth.

Darkly slid her hand under the girl's arm.

"Come on. I'll take you to my room where you can rest. I'll find your uncle. He'll be happy to see you," Darkly whispered and helped Marielle to her feet.

Marielle was in no position to argue. She was broken and at the mercy of a stronger will. Darkly guided her into her room and to the bed. The exhausted girl collapsed into sleep. When Darkly covered Marielle with the dusty blanket, she flailed in her sleep, fighting off an imaginary force. Darkly copied what her adoptive mother did when she woke to night terrors. She placed her hand over Marielle's heart. As their breathing synchronized, so did the terror subside.

Darkly sat on the edge of the bed and stared out the window across the dark and silent town.

"What the hell happened here?" she asked herself.

Darkly changed her gaze, traveling across the river and up to the look-out ridge where both her mother and father lost their lives, albeit years apart. It was then she noticed the flicker. Like the split-second flash of light from a bug zapper. Darkly got up, walked to the window and stuck her head out into the night air. There it was again. A flicker. Two flickers. Darkly wondered if it could be a campfire. A family enjoying a warm night by a quaint forest town full of monsters?

Darkly waded across the ford in the river. She'd left Marielle sleeping like the dead. She'd witnessed that kind of sleep before. A constable comes in from a weeks' long cold trek, and they generally don't get out of bed for two or three days. Marielle wasn't going anywhere.

Darkly ducked into tree cover and climbed up to a spot alongside the dirt road that put her about a quarter of a mile from the summit and that yet-to-be-identified flicker. In the dense wood, she had no choice but to use her flashlight. The beam bounced off the chrome of a hubcap. The hubcap was attached to a deflated tire, and as Darkly moved the light upwards, she saw that the tire was attached to an RV.

The vehicle was permanently listing, wedged between two clumps of birch trees. Vines and nettles had grown up and over the camper and through its broken windows. At Darkly's feet, a covering of tiny white paint chips imitated snow. The metal walls of the last home she lived in with her parents had turned to rust.

Darkly attempted to part the growth of branches that blocked her way inside the door to the RV. It was no use. She would have needed a saw to succeed. So, she walked around the perimeter of the vehicle and found the front windshield intact. She didn't want to bring attention to herself. Noise carries far in these parts. But, for Darkly, this couldn't wait. Surely the seals around the window would give way without too much effort?

Darkly climbed up a tree that draped itself over the front of the RV. She locked one foot between two boughs, grabbed hold of a branch with her two hands, and then placed her free foot against the glass. She applied gentle pressure at first, and then bore down with most of her weight. Just as she thought. One end of the windshield popped free like a lens in a pair of sunglasses.

Darkly hopped out of the tree and pulled her Inuit knife from the sheath strapped to her leg. She slid the blade under the window and cut the weathered strip of sealant. She then grabbed hold of an end and pulled it away from the glass like pulling apart string cheese. Darkly caught the pane of glass before it fell to the ground, and propped it up against the tree. Here she was. Home.

Darkly grabbed ahold of the steering wheel and pulled herself into the vehicle. The driver's seat was now a petri dish of mold. She steadied herself into a slanted upright position by pressing her fingers into the roof, which was closing in on the floor after two decades of vegetation pulling the RV into the ground.

It was a mess. Another Chernobyl. Yet, like that toxic town reclaimed by the Ukrainian wilderness, there were still signs of the RV's former humanity present. Darkly shone her light across the breakfast nook and into the storage space below the seat. The place she hid from her own kind. Darkly's mother, Catharine, flashed across her mind. The yellow seeping into the eyes, as she became the monster she wished above all other things to save Darkly from.

Darkly felt a moment of guilt. She had betrayed her mother's final commandment. She felt the empty space above her chest, where the silver amulet had been a permanent fixture up until a few days ago.

Darkly looked over at the cupboards. Most of them were closed. The kitchenette was intact. A bottle of propane and a scrub brush, and Darkly could make a meal in it. She didn't know why, but she felt compelled to open one of the cupboards. Inside, she found faded, water-stained polaroids pinned to the wood. They were of Darkly. The locales were all tourist spots on the Family Stewart's last holiday. There was Darkly standing in front of the door to a motel room shaped like a teepee. There was Darkly in front of the Canadian border crossing. There as Darkly crouching slightly and pressing her head up into the hand of a sasquatch statue.

It was during the mixture of grief, regret and nostalgia fighting for first place within Darkly, that she discovered she was singing. Well, humming, with the occasional lyric she could remember. Some Tina Turner song about children who couldn't find their way back home. It was then that the hand of long leathery fingers reached in through a broken window and grabbed her jacket.

Darkly almost jumped inside the cupboard.

CHAPTER THREE

Snow is a book that rewrites itself each time it falls. William was reading the story it had to tell this incarnation. The large feet and the comparatively small paws met at the place William knelt over. No longer was one set tracking the other. This was a dance. A violent dance that ended with the large feet the only prints to carry on walking.

William scanned the horizon ahead. No sign of a body. That could only mean it was carried away. Alive or dead, William wondered? Alive was preferable. He was certain he was tracking the serial killer. The trapper, Deluche. There was no doubt after the last slaughter. He thought about the mother and her two children and buried the sorrow he felt for two young lives that would never truly know life.

William had tried to give his wife, Elizabeth, a child from the first night of their marriage. Several years later, she was eating mood pills in place of meals and reading about fertility treatment miracles in Reader's Digest.

The young Mountie pushed the thoughts of new life from his mind and thought about what he may have to do. He had killed a suspect before. When there was absolute certainty of guilt and he knew it was him or them. But, to bring a murderer back to face trial by the people he left to corrupt an unspoiled wilderness, that was the prize every man who came before William longed for. If Deluche was still alive, William would do everything in his power to keep it that way. The reality, of course, was that there would need to be some kind of unfortunate accident arranged before Deluche stood trial, but after he and William's photograph were on every front page across the country. A warning to more of his kind. It goes without saying, there is a protocol to follow when bringing in a werewolf.

For the Inuit communities, a people who had endured every known hardship inflicted upon man, there was no need to protect them from the truth. They did not hide themselves from reality behind central heating and popular entertainment that turned monsters into mythology. Constables would spread the word. The shapeshifter is dead. Your women and children are safe.

William set out again, following the lonely set of impossibly big tracks, and asking himself if another legend was true.

William trudged along the barren stretch of wilderness all day, following the tracks, plain as day in the snow and a couple of inches deeper than the indentations his own boots were creating. Still, there was nothing in sight yet.

Then, slowly, like the sun rising over water, something dark and low to the ground grew in size with every step William took. With the flatness of the terrain, it was not long before he could pick out the form of a body. A flap of leather and long, black, stringy hair blew in the wind. That's all that was moving.

It became quickly apparent that William was not the only being approaching the body. Making its way from the opposite direction, and sure to get there before William, was a polar bear. For an animal with no qualms about hunting humans, William pondered for a split second if such an easy meal was in any way disappointing to the creature.

William pulled his rifle out of the pack on his back and took aim at the bear's head. He was too far to guarantee accuracy, so he began running towards the bear. Well, the bear ran. Its paws were designed for it. The snow was compacted enough, that William didn't need his snowshoes. But, this wasn't a suburban jogging route. William's feet in snow, however hard, were not going to cover ground with any significant speed. Plus, William had his sweat to contend with. Work up too much heat, and he'd have clothes to dry out.

This was going to be close. The bear was just ten seconds from its willing prey. William slid into a kneeling position. Nine. He raised the rifle. Eight. He found the bear's moving head in his sight. Seven. The polar bear was galloping, causing its tongue to flap from cheek to cheek. It was salivating. Six. Let it get a little closer. Five. Take the safety off. Four. Finger on the trigger. Three. Fire.

Two. The bullet found its way into the brain of the bear, and the animal's forward momentum kept it moving. The head went down, and then the front legs. The torso fell over the head. One. The polar bear did a summersault and landed inches from the body of another natural killer.

William slid the rifle back into his pack, got up and walked the remaining distance to the bear. One of its front paws was touching the head of the man it had almost eaten for a meal. He was a tall man, muscular and wiry. He was dressed in a hide tunic and pants. Remarkably, he was alive, but hypothermia had set in. William had little time to act.

The Mountie pulled a knife from a belt around his leg and thrust the point into the polar bear's navel. With extreme effort, William sawed his way up to the ribs of the bear. He turned his head away, while he pulled the skin and muscle apart. The guts fell out onto William's prisoner. He covered the man with internal organs. They would not retain their heat long.

The next morning, William emerged from his pup tent. The unconscious serial killer was weak, but alive, and recovering in a Mountie-issue sleeping bag. William had stripped down naked and kept his suspect alive with body warmth. He had taken the opportunity to perform a physical examination. The man's back was broken. Someone or something had broken him in two, carried him across the arctic and then left him to die from exposure. Retribution, clearly. But, delivered from who?

William knew the killer would heal quickly. His kind did. So, he'd keep the man tranquilized and carry him out of the wilderness on a litter of ice and rope. William lit his can of sterno and began melting ice in a tin cup. It was then that he saw it. In the distance. A large brown bear on two legs. Only, it wasn't a bear.

Darkly had never run so fast in her life. She sprang on two legs out from the trees and into the clearing that overlooked the Moon river. There, before Darkly, were the torches she saw flickering from a distance, and Wyatt, whose legs and arms were tied to two tree trunks rammed into the ground to form a letter X.

Wyatt looked up, shaking away the sweat, blood, and hair that blocked his vision.

"Whatever you do, don't sing," he said weakly, and then passed out.

Darkly turned and pointed her gun into the forest. That is how she stood until dawn.

Darkly studied the giant footprint a few feet into the forest. A bare footprint. An extremely large, bare footprint. A bear? One bear following in the footsteps of another? She turned for a split second to check on Wyatt. The hairs on the back of her head leapt to attention, and her head shot back around to face nothing. There had been a puff of breath on the back her neck. She was losing it. She had to pull herself together and figure out what happened in the last few days.

Darkly walked over to Wyatt and cut him down. Her mouth was afire with the killer's infliction of death. He collapsed unconscious to the ground. She'd need a vehicle to get him back to town. Fortunately, the Korean War jeep that the film crew had shuttled around town in was abandoned along with the crew circus of trailers and gear. Twist a couple wires together, and Darkly had her gurney.

It was morning when Darkly pulled Wyatt into bed and threw the dusty bedspread over his body. Marielle, who had been wandering the halls like a specter, peered around the door. She then became fascinated with the door frame, running her fingers along it, recollecting her past through touch.

"Do you want to keep an eye on him for me?"

Marielle withdrew from Darkly's sight for a moment, then stepped fully into the frame.

"Come get me when he wakes up? I'll find us some food at the diner."

Marielle nodded her head and sat down cross-legged on the bed. She began a staring contest with the comatose psychopath, while Darkly began her investigation.

In the town, Darkly found meals left on tables, now feasts for flies. Drawers of clothes were dumped on beds. The air in the abandoned homes was charged with fear, like the moments before a storm, when God appears over the horizon, falling to earth in flashes of brilliance and rivers of destruction.

Darkly also searched Buck's office. Paperwork and file folders were strewn across the floor. The rifles missing from the cabinet that was the town's arsenal. Doc's surgery was wiped clean of any useful item. This was an immediate exodus. Panic. A last resort. She gathered up the paperwork and settled herself into Buck's swivel chair. There had to be some indication of what had transpired after the night of her escape. If not in what she examined before her, in what might be missing.

The papers were a jumble, though Darkly quickly learned that the type of paper corresponded to the year it was made use of. Yellowed paper the thickness of onion skin came from the days before Buck assumed the role of sheriff. She looked over at the manual typewriter consigned to the end of Buck's desk and then at the letter *B* that adorned the corners of many of the pages. Buck was a meticulous man.

It was late morning when Darkly had begun sifting through the records of domestic squabbles, livestock deaths, and updates to town statutes. Now, with lunchtime behind her, she was getting hungry and finding it difficult to concentrate. She needed to eat, as did Marielle. And maybe Wyatt.

Darkly gathered the paperwork up and shoved it into a leather bag she found in Buck's desk and made her way to the Moon River Diner. She could study Buck's records better over a full stomach.

She took a look back at Buck's desk, as the door was shutting behind her. Darkly found herself longing for the sheriff. One her way back to Wolf Woods, Buck had become the new foundation of normalcy in her mind. He was to be the center of a new world she would belong to. A world she had always belonged to but just not known it.

The diner was, from all appearances, abandoned like the homes of the townsfolk. The diner counter had half-empty glasses of water sitting on it. Darkly stepped behind the counter to examine a lone beef patty on the grill. She pushed her index finger into the partially-cooked meat and smelled it. It wasn't worth taking the chance, so she moved on to the refrigerator.

Devastation greeted her when she turned the corner. The floor was covered in broken glass from jars of preserves. Among the sparkling shards, were pickled onions, gherkins, preserved peaches and gooseberries. But, there was something else. She thought it was jam at first. Or was it ketchup? Where the vinegar from the jars pooled in places, like lakes on a map, this substance had dried a brownish hue. She flaked it with her fingernail. This was blood. A trail of blood.

Darkly stood back. She needed a more aerial view to distinguish the blood from the edible debris. The counter next to the sink full of dirty dishes would do. She pushed more dishes into the water, disturbing the layer of scum that had formed on the top, and lifted herself up.

Darkly focused on the brown drips and smears, and the way they spread themselves out across the floor. A pattern emerged of rows of five smudges moving in a flock towards the walk-in refrigerator. They were toes.

She hopped off the counter and tip-toed through the minefield to examine the toe marks more closely. In a couple she could make out the rings of toe prints. The widths from big toe drip to little toe drip was almost a foot wide.

Darkly looked up at the walk-in. She followed the prints until they disappeared under the door. She placed her cheek to the surface of the door. It was cool. The lights were on in the diner, as they were in Buck's office. So, generators were still going strong for the two hearts of the town.

"Hello?" she called.

What was she thinking? If someone had crawled in here more than a few hours ago, they would have died of hypothermia by now. Darkly reached for the handle.

CRASH. Something heavy slammed up against the door from the inside, knocking Darkly onto her ass from the shock of it. A glass shard dug into her thigh. She stifled her scream with her hand.

"Shit."

Darkly looked around her for a clear spot of floor to plant her palms on the ground and lift herself back up. She pulled the shard of glass from her flesh and placed it silently on the floor, while not taking her eyes off the refrigerator door. Then she stood there, waiting for the next crash. It didn't come.

What if that was the last desperate action of someone on the verge of succumbing to hypothermia? Well surely, she corrected herself, a local would have turned to wolf to stave off the cold. That would explain the power behind that door. A big wolf from the look of the prints on the floor. She couldn't just leave them to starve to death, and behind that door may be the answer to what happened to Buck and everyone else in Wolf Woods.

She reached for the handle without hesitation, stepped to the side, out of the way of whoever would come charging out, placed her free hand on her gun, and swung open the door. But, once again, she waited for nothing. Ten seconds passed before she drew her gun and peered around the door.

The light from the diner revealed the walk-in's contents. A side of beef hung in the center of the small room, and the walls were lined with jars of fruits, vegetables, and unidentifiable ingredients. The floor was littered with torn burlap, onions, potatoes and strips of fatty bacon. A turnip came rolling from a dark corner of the walk-in, and Darkly took the safety off her gun. She inched her way toward the corner, where burlap bags were stacked one on top of the other. She kicked the lowest bag. The top bag toppled down, and turnips scattered across the floor. Nothing was hiding there.

At that moment, the sound of destruction erupted from the restaurant. Darkly rushed out to see tables and chairs lying where they had been thrown against the walls of the diner. And a seven-foot pane of glass, upon which the words *Moon River* had been painted, lay in smithereens on the ground outside. It wasn't just a big wolf. It was a quick one. Too quick to be seen. What the hell?

Darkly set the burlap bag down at the foot of the bed. She reached in, pulled out a jar of string beans and handed it to Marielle, who twisted the lid off immediately and began devouring the beans several at a time.

Wyatt was still asleep. Darkly slapped him hard across the face. He didn't stir. She sighed and took a seat on the floor next to Marielle and opened a jar of peaches. Marielle took the briefest of breaks between shoving her mouth with beans to speak.

"He's infected. He'll die."

"How do you know?" asked Darkly.

"You can tell from the color of his skin. Blue."

Darkly looked up at Wyatt. She stood up and went to the window to open the curtains fully. With the increased light, Darkly could make out the blue tinge around his pale nostrils, eye sockets and lips.

"What is he infected with, Marielle?"

"Silver," Marielle replied with the satisfaction of a full stomach.

"How did he become infected?"

Marielle set down the now empty jar and climbed up onto the bed. She pulled the covers off Wyatt and pulled his shirt up over his face. She traced her fingers along his stomach and chest, then rolled him over onto his back and repeated the examination. Then, she proceeded to strip Wyatt naked and work her way down to the soles of his feet.

Marielle was stumped. She sat next to Wyatt's prone body, clearly thinking hard. Already, this was not the mindless waif Darkly found wandering the hotel. Then, Marielle sprang back to life, and grabbed Wyatt's head so forcefully that Darkly thought his neck would snap. She ran her fingertips through Wyatt's hair, picking apart the strands like a preening monkey to examine the scalp. Then, she peered inside his left ear, and whipped his head around to examine the right ear. She looked into Darkly's eyes. Bingo.

Darkly grabbed Wyatt's head and looked into his ear. There was a silver ball. She hooked the ball with her fingernail and pulled it out. The ball was on a string and connected to another ball and then another ball and then another ball. Darkly removed a strand of bloodied silver beads from Wyatt's ear with the help of a hand-kerchief. The simple square of fabric had proven as useful to her work as a gun. When the last bead was free, Wyatt gasped once and returned to his deathly quiet state.

Darkly examined the beads closely. There were engraved characters on the beads. A raven, a wolf, a moon, and a distorted human mask.

"It's Haida art."

Marielle touched her fingertip to one of the beads and recoiled in pain.

"A shaman's weapon against werewolves."

She looked down at Wyatt and scowled.

"You should put them back, Darkly."

As much as she would have liked to, Darkly didn't follow Marielle's advice.

CHAPTER FOUR

Darkly searched through Buck's records. There had to be something about the town's relations with the local First Nations tribe. Marielle was asleep in a corner of the room, covered in a blanket. Wyatt, the color returning to his face, was sleeping soundly in the next room. The fact Darkly could hear his snoring indicated to Darkly more than anything else that he was on the mend. Marielle had told her the first thing Wyatt would do after waking was turn to hunt. God help anyone who crossed his path in those hours.

So, Darkly felt distance was best for all. But, not too much distance. The thought had occurred to her to kill Wyatt or at least re-insert the beads until she had a better grasp of the situation. He deserved death after all the suffering he had inflicted on others, including her own family. But, her instincts told her he had a part yet to play in all this. She could always kill him later. The taste of death had waned in Wyatt's and Marielle's presence. A natural desensitization she welcomed. Darkly had experienced it before with a trigger-happy instructor she couldn't avoid during her academy days.

The paperwork was far from engrossing reading. Buck seemed to relish the bureaucratic element of running a self-imposed prison state. Most of his notes were about rationing, patrols of the town's boundaries and chasing off curious hikers. Marielle's name caught her eye. What followed was a decidedly unemotional half-page account of a young woman being told to leave the only home she had ever known and to never come back. Buck's notes indicated she had been chosen as one of those who would lay the groundwork for *exodus*. What Buck described as *her aggressive interest in sex* made Marielle an ideal candidate. That was it. Darkly could find only brief references to exodus in the other papers.

There was no mystery in the meaning. Exodus means leaving. A town that could no longer provide mates for its young people had to kidnap outsiders, as they did with Darkly and the film crew. Or, their young people must set out to find mates, and create new wolves and safe homes for future colonists. But, what would inspire an entire town to evacuate? The old, the sick, the infants. All of them gone.

Darkly ran the Haida beads in the handkerchief between her thumb and fingers. Wyatt was defeated and left to rot on the hilltop. So, no threat there. Something happened in a very short space of time that forced Buck to lead his people out of Wolf Woods. Darkly suddenly realized that the snoring next door had stopped.

She placed her ear to the wall and then crossed to the window. Below it, a wolf looked up at her, then turned and ran for the river. Wyatt crossed the ford and disappeared into the trees on the other side.

Sing, thought Darkly. Don't sing, to be precise. What did Wyatt mean? And would he come back to her after hunting? He would. She couldn't explain why, but of that she had no doubt. The wind blew in through the window. A storm was brewing. The draft blew her stack of papers across the room.

As she collected the records once again, she found it. A Haida sketch. A sketch that matched the mask on one of the beads. An angry man. No, bloodthirsty man? Well, that surely described the good people of Wolf Woods. Around the mask were little stars. They formed an arch over and to the sides of the mask. The sky? She looked out the window at the dimming light. Maybe. But, the drawing reminded her of something.

Darkly leaned her head out the window and watched the clouds roll in and cover the brightest stars in the galaxy that were beginning to shine. She looked out over the quiet streets and then turned her attention to the Moon River and followed its winding way until it disappeared around a corner in the forest. She ducked back in and grabbed the sketch. Of course. The cave of bones. The one filled with faux diamonds that shone like the night sky. The First Nations tomb.

The sun had completely fallen when Darkly crossed the ford in the Moon River. The light rain made a soothing sound as it hit the pebbles around her. The pebbles would soon be covered, as the water level rose in the storm. She climbed onto the bank and began the trek along the river. Darkly pulled the hood of her jacket up over her head and wiped the damp from her cheeks. She looked back at the dark shadows of buildings across the river and then pointed her flashlight into the sheet of water that was falling heavier by the second.

The bank grew muddy, slowing Darkly's way. It was an hour later when she reached the entrance to the cave. Half of the boards had been ripped away since she had last been here. There was room enough for a large bear to climb inside, and Darkly had only to duck to escape the rain.

She stood right by the entrance and kneeled to examine the ground for prints. What could have been a toe and the edge of a heel and even a dog print were barely noticeable in the fine dust that covered the rock of the cave floor. Darkly pointed her flashlight at the cave walls ahead, catching the glint of the semi-precious flecks of stone embedded within. She took a few steps and then a few more. She reached the point where she had fallen during her last visit. It was still littered with bones. Beyond that, she reached a fork in the cave. To the left, a tunnel appeared to narrow and grow smaller, whereas to the right, the cave seemed to open up into a gallery. She took the right fork.

Darkly walked for a couple of minutes, slowly shuffling down the natural corridor. As she moved forward, the walls expanded, and the ceiling continued to open up. The little stars were now visible in the rock below her feet. She was surrounded. It was as though she was on a spacewalk.

Then the walls and ceiling gave way completely, and she found herself in the middle of a large rock bubble. The rock above her head was pockmarked with openings. She could tell this because her head became the occasional target of showers that dried up the moment she took another step and then resumed on the next step.

She scanned the gallery with her flashlight. It was about one hundred feet across. The floor was treacherous, smooth rock polished by running water. Something caught her eye in the center of the gallery. Something white. She made her way gingerly along the slick rock towards the object. It was clothing or a blanket. It was a sheet. Darkly could see it was stained, and that it covered a pile of objects. She reached down to pull the sheet away. It was then that a prolonged shriek cut through her skin and bone. It bounced off the cave walls, so that Darkly couldn't tell what direction it was coming from.

Darkly raised her gun, not knowing where to point it. She began spinning and lost her footing, tripping over the sheet and pulling it free from what it had been covering. Bones. Most stripped clean of flesh. Human bones. This she knew because the head was very much intact. Staring back at her was Christopher, the actor killed soon after she first arrived at Wolf Woods, supposedly by a bear. This cave was a place of offerings. A place to feed! Who was doing the eating?

Of course, she had since learned from Buck that Christopher was not really an actor. He was a native of Wolf Woods bringing fresh DNA back to his hometown in order to refresh the gene pool and gain forgiveness for past sins. Christopher had been a meal for something. The shriek she heard did not sound like any bear she'd heard before. Darkly knew it was time to get out of there.

She got to her feet only to feel something powerful hit her in the chest and send her onto her back, and sliding along the wet rock away from the center of the gallery. She managed to hold onto her gun, but the flashlight rolled away from her reach. Darkly pointed the gun up and fired a warning shot into the darkness. All was quiet, except for the pitter patter of rain on rock. Her heart was racing, but she slowed her breathing and focused her eyes on the blackness for movement. Her training enabled her to find a path through panic.

Just as her senses were becoming attuned to her environment, she was knocked off guard again, when the most ungodly stench entered her nostrils. Then a hand grabbed one of her ankles and dragged her across the width of the gallery at remarkable speed. Whoever had ahold of her began racing around the perimeter of the gallery slamming her upper body into the rock.

Darkly had seconds to react before she would surely lose con-sciousness. She let off several rounds into the darkness. Without seeing, she found her target. The unholy shriek that filled the cav-ern was no human and no wolf. Darkly was free.

She leapt to her feet and ran along the edge of the rock wall until finding a turn in the rock. She followed it, never letting her fingertips lose contact. The pressure in her ears told her that the walls were closing in. She was back in the tunnel. A minute later, and she would be at the cave entrance. She ran through the agony that was filling her mouth…down to the roots of her teeth.

Then Darkly heard it. The snorting and snarling. Her attacker was behind her. It may be wounded, but it was gaining ground. She could make out a change in light ahead. Less darkness. Then she went flying face first into the ground and felt her chin burst open upon the sandy ground. She'd forgotten about the rock step.

There was no time to feel the pain. Darkly got up on her elbows and crawled to the broken boards and flung herself out into the open air, diving down the river bank and landing at the feet of an old Indian man dressed in a long leather overcoat and a cowboy hat.

"Something's after me." Darkly pleaded, hoping the man was on her side.

The old man looked directly into the cave entrance and sang. It was low and guttural. Throat singing. Darkly had heard it on a trip to the arctic. It was primeval. It was mesmerizing. She looked behind her at the cave. There stood the outline of a man. At least she thought it was a man. An impossibly large man, who must have been three times her size. She turned back to look up at the old Indian just in time to see the end of a staff slam into the side of her head.

CHAPTER FIVE

Darkly smelled the burning, then heard the crackle of fire. She was still mostly asleep, but in that weird state where she was alert enough to know she was asleep. In her mind, she was in her childhood bedroom, and the walls were catching fire. The flames were melting the wallpaper and plaster, so that it pooled on the floor, rising in waves that threatened to engulf Darkly's bed.

Darkly opened her eyes. She immediately saw the smoke and sat straight up. It was then she felt the pain in her head. The throbbing guided her fingers to the pronounced bump under her hair, and the memories of last night came back to her. At least she assumed it was last night. Maybe she'd been out longer than that.

She looked around her. It was a hut. A weave of branches, whose holes were stuffed with moss. In the center of the roof, a hole released smoke from a small fire in a pit in the ground. Darkly was lying on animal pelts a few feet from the pit. Just inside the edge of the pit were two white eggs. Underneath her head, was a moose bladder filled with water and doubling as a pillow. Darkly removed the cork and took a drink. It was warm, sweet, not unpleasant. But, it wasn't water. The interior of the small hut became cloudy, and Darkly swore she could see water droplets hanging still in the air around her. She collapsed back onto the animal skins.

Darkly turned her face toward the fire and watched as, remarkably, one of the two eggs rolled up out of the pit and cracked open. Darkly witnessed a fully-grown raven emerge from the egg, fly up into the air, then land back on the dirt ground in the form of a girl.

Surface veins covered the naked girl's body like the veins of a leaf or the varicose veins in an old person's legs. The purplish lines covered her face, her arms, her small breasts. The girl looked at Darkly, but didn't look at her. Her eyes were best described as looking inward. Her body jerked and her face twitched. She jutted her hand out at Darkly, who wanted to recoil, but now found herself paralyzed. The girl brushed her fingertips down Darkly's face and whispered, "Sing."

Whispered was not exactly right. Clucked was more apt. The word came out of the girl's throat, but her lips did not move. The girl suddenly cocked her head and turned and hobbled away from Darkly. She spread her arms and was a raven again, flying up through the smoke hole in the top of the hut, the embers from the fire singeing the feathers of her wings.

Darkly bolted upright to face the old Indian man from outside the cave. He was seated cross-legged on the ground on the other side of the now dying fire. He was eating a hardboiled egg. He pointed at the other egg, still sitting on the edge of the small fire pit. That was some First Nations drug-induced magic.

"Duck egg," he said.

"Where am I?" Darkly asked.

"In the forest," replied the old man.

He grabbed the remaining egg and tapped it on a stone. He then peeled the shell and passed it to Darkly.

"What was that I drank?" Darkly asked without taking the egg.

"Medicine."

"I'm not sick."

"Are you sure? Maybe you are hungry then?"

Darkly took the egg and bit into it, examining the inside. It appeared to be just an egg. She finished it.

"Why did you attack me?"

Darkly didn't know whether she was a guest or a prisoner. The old man smiled.

"I had to show him you weren't a threat. In case he came out of the cave. It was raining pretty hard. But I couldn't take the chance."

"Him?"

"My grandfather."

This from a man who was seventy if a day. Darkly was certain she could take the man if he forced her to. She just needed to stay clear of his stick. But, he wasn't all with it. If his grandfather was genuinely alive, he'd be at least 120 years old. This guy was a hermit, she guessed. Someone alone in the woods for far too long and in such dire need of company, he'll kidnap it if he has to.

The old man pointed at the faint blue spider veins on Darkly's neck.

"You're a wolf. But trapped."

Now Darkly was getting somewhere.

"You know the people of Wolf Woods?"

"The enemies of my ancestors. Stole their hunting grounds. Starved my grandfather. He changed."

Maybe she wasn't getting anywhere, Darkly reassessed.

"Have you seen the sheriff? Sheriff Buck?"

At this question, the old man got up and made his way to the draped skin that led to the outside.

"The bird will follow you now. Keep watch over you."

"No, please wait. I'm trying to find my friends. They've disappeared. The whole town has vanished. I'm an RCMP constable on official business."

31

The old man stepped out of the hut and let the hide fall down behind him. Darkly followed him out. But he was gone. He had disappeared into thin air.

Marielle heard Wyatt's voice. Like all canines, she could sense fear. It had a frequency that filled the head with the instinct to take advantage of weakness and claim an easy meal.

"Hello," he called. "Is anyone here? Can someone tell me where I am?"

Marielle looked out the window. The warm sun hit her face. It was a beautiful face. She was rejuvenated. Two days of rest and recuperation, as well as the healing powers of her kind, had reduced the burns to faint scars. There was one thing, though. A condition that came with permanent change and everlasting repercussions. She was pregnant. She was completely sure of it. She guessed it was the kid in the toilet stall on the night she met Darkly. She had wanted to kill Darkly that night. Now, her feelings had taken another direction.

Marielle watched Wyatt walk past the church and the sheriff's station. He was stark naked. Here was another change in Marielle. She had always had an insatiable appetite for the opposite sex. She had left home as much to set her desires free as she had to fulfill the mission to give her people a future. Not to mention her confrontations with other young women in Wolf Woods who held back their affections to acquire commitment. Marielle was what they labeled *easy*. They had made life in a small town unbearable for Marielle.

But, where the sight of a man as well-endowed as Wyatt would have required immediate satisfaction for her cravings in the past, Marielle's inclinations were evolving. In the night, her dreams had turned erotic, as they often did. She had felt the one hand pinching her breast, teasing her with a little pain, while the other hand brushed its fingers lightly between her legs before plunging inside of her. She gasped and opened her eyes within her dream to see Darkly's face looking back at her.

What was Wyatt playing at? From what she had heard about him, walking naked through town was something he would find amusing. If he had an audience. There was no audience today. And then there was what Marielle surmised to be fear. Wyatt sat down in the middle of the road and cried. The fear was genuine. This was most peculiar behavior for a psycho.

Darkly made her way through the trees toward the sound of running water. By looking for moss on the trees, she was able to point herself in the right direction and let the river guide her back to town. She passed the old mine shaft entrance to the cave system about an hour after setting off. It had been re-boarded up. By the old Indian, she guessed.

Back in town, Darkly stopped in at the diner and grabbed a few more jars of pickled foods and then headed back to the hotel.

After the few days she'd had, she wasn't particularly surprised to find Wyatt and Marielle in the lobby. Wyatt was dressed in nothing but a towel wrapped around his waist. He was devouring what she would soon learn was his fifth raw potato.

"He doesn't know who he is," Marielle explained and then introduced Darkly. "Wyatt, this is Darkly."

Wyatt took a pause from eating and nodded his head. Darkly looked into his eyes in search of the serial killer and the man who brutally murdered Peter and Shane. She saw what Marielle sensed. Her training enabled her to separate liars from honest men. This man's mind was lost. Darkly began her questioning.

"Do you know your name?"

Wyatt pointed at Marielle.

"She told me it's Wyatt."

"Does it sound familiar to you?" Darkly continued.

"No," Wyatt replied.

"Okay. Well, I can confirm that you do go by the name Wyatt. What's your first memory, Wyatt?"

"Waking up."

"Where were you?"

"In the woods. I was naked."

"Did you know where to go when you woke up?"

"I saw the town. I was on a hill."

Wyatt went back to eating, and Darkly stepped away, calling Marielle over to her with a nod of the head.

"Does he know what he is?" Darkly whispered to Marielle.

"He probably senses something. Those silver beads are to blame. They were in his brain."

Darkly looked back at Wyatt, who had finished the fifth potato and was working on a sixth. She looked back at Marielle and finally clocked into the fact the girl's body was healed. More than healed, she was *new*. Marielle's cloudy mind seemed to have cleared fully, as well.

"You're doing better."

"I'm pregnant."

"That's quite the glow."

Darkly didn't know what else to say to that, so she turned her attention back to Wyatt, who looked up at her approach.

"Wyatt, we're in the dark like you. Our friends who lived here disappeared. We don't know where they've gone. But, somewhere locked in your mind, is the answer to that mystery. So, I would like to try and help you remember. After you've finished eating."

"Okay."

At that, Wyatt stood up and let the towel fall to the floor.

"We should first get you some clothes," Darkly suggested.

Though of different builds, Wyatt and Buck were of similar height. Where Buck was more solid, Wyatt was wirier. So, with a belt and a rolling up of sleeves, Wyatt fit into his forgotten brother's clothes.

Darkly took Wyatt on a tour of the home he grew up in, but nothing jogged the man's memory. Black and white photos of his parents and his brother didn't cut through the fog. His whole life had been misplaced. Understanding that the sense of smell was the greatest inducer of memory recall, Darkly had Wyatt sniff Buck's clothes, the furniture, the bedding, the moose jerky in Buck's cupboard, which he was also happy to taste. Not a recollection found its way out into the open. With this place being the closest to Wyatt's childhood development, she was forced to ponder the likelihood that Wyatt's brain had been permanently damaged by the silver beads, and that whoever inserted them, knew they were taking away a man's identity.

A despicable human being's identity, Darkly had to remind herself. But, Darkly's job was not to judge criminals. It was to bring them to the judge. Was this a sentence that had befallen Wyatt? Had Buck defeated him? Then, unable to bring himself to kill his own flesh and fur, Wyatt was condemned to lose his identity and wander the woods a lost soul?

And what about that warning word, *sing*? The spouting off from a deranged mind on the edge of oblivion, then recollected later by Darkly in her high state? Occam's razor made the simplest explanation the most probable. But, what about the cave? Sensory deprivation and a wily old man who was quite handy with his wooden staff and bag of potions was the most reasoned conclusion.

Darkly proceeded to march Wyatt to every building in the town, trying to jog his memory. Doc's home, the church, the homes of people Wyatt would have grown up with and would have known as well as any flesh and blood relative. Hell, thought Darkly, they were all flesh and blood by now in this incestuous town.

At the orphan Lily's home, they took a break. In the cellar, next to the sandbox of root vegetables and the pots of coveted beetroot sugar, Darkly found a couple dozen small brown bottles of home-made ale. The three investigators enjoyed cellar temperature beer under a sun that was drying up the wet ground. It was out in the vegetable garden that Darkly first noticed the prints. A child's feet.

In a small puddle of muddy water, Darkly made out the shallow imprint of little toes. She followed them down to the fence of the sheep paddock. The animals had since been let loose, scattered across the hillsides, to be picked off one-by-one by coyotes.

But, within the past three days, a child had walked up to the wooden fence Darkly now looked over to check on her flock. Darkly looked down. On the other side of the fence, facing the tiny feet, were two large bare footprints.

Darkly interpreted the events that followed. The small footprints turned and moved down the fence line, but only for a short distance. After about ten feet, the large footprints replaced the smaller ones, as though they had eaten them up. The prints ended abruptly and reappeared on the other side of the fence. Darkly followed them halfway across the field, and then turned to Marielle.

"Who else in this town had children? Young children who would have been old enough to play on their own outside?"

Marielle thought for a minute.

"Maybe six or seven families. Not many."

"Take me to their homes," Darkly ordered.

Darkly stepped onto the creaking boards of the back porch. The home was in the center of town, just a few doors down from the church. Beyond the backyard, the quietest of neighbors could be found six feet under in the Wolf Woods cemetery.

She had visited this home previously before she knew what she was looking for. She had raced through, looking for signs of evacuation or for those who may have been abandoned and remained in hiding.

Darkly walked past the dishes in the sink, and the wooden truck on the kitchen table. She passed into the family's sitting room, with Marielle and Wyatt close on her heels. There was an old-fashioned radio in one corner and a sofa covered in quilts backed up against one wall, that faced a staircase leading up to the second story.

In another corner, was a wood stove. A tea kettle sat on top. Darkly picked up the kettle and inspected the bottom, which was brittle, its metal compromised by prolonged exposure to the heat. The stove still radiated a tiny amount of warmth.

Next to the stove, was what Darkly was looking for. An aluminum bathtub. Big enough to fit an adult. It was filled with water. Almost to the top. Enough water that a child could get in just barely without the water overflowing.

"It was raining pretty hard," she said to herself, remembering the words of the old Indian.

Darkly looked around the base of the tub. She then got on her hands and knees and pressed her face to the floor.

"What are you looking for?" queried Marielle.

"I'll know when I see it," answered Darkly.

Darkly's eyes took her to the sofa and something poking out from underneath. She reached under and pulled a short metal pipe out from where it conceivably could have rolled. Darkly studied it and the bathtub.

Darkly handed the pipe to Marielle and took off her jacket. She then removed her top and her jeans, and then her boots and her socks.

"What are you doing?" asked the normally silent Wyatt.

He was eating a piece of bread he had found in the kitchen. It looked moldy.

"I need to test a theory," replied Darkly, and kept undressing.

She took it all off. Wyatt kept eating, and Marielle accepted Darkly's most intimate of intimates. Neither seemed at all phased.

Darkly then dipped her fingers in the water in the bathtub.

"Not too chilly," Darkly said hopefully.

She then put one foot in and then the other. She stood there, like the fully-grown Venus emerging from a metal oyster. Darkly reached her hand out to Marielle, who then began to remove her shoes.

"No. I meant pass me the pipe." Darkly smiled.

"Oh."

Marielle handed Darkly the pipe, and Darkly sat down in the tub, disguising the shock of the coolness of the water on her naked skin with tightly closed lips and a brief hum. Water splashed out onto the floor, causing Wyatt and Marielle to step back.

Darkly took a breath and laid back into the tub, submerging her whole body below the water and holding herself in position with her feet pressed against metal. She brought an end of the pipe to her mouth and blew out, clearing the pipe of any water. She then breathed in. And then out. She breathed comfortably, slowing her heartrate, which had elevated at the anticipation of being deprived of oxygen. She looked up at Marielle and Wyatt peering over the top of the tub.

Marielle reached into the water and took Darkly's hand. The pregnancy had made her hormonal, Darkly thought.

After a couple of minutes underwater, Darkly reemerged. She sat there for a moment, thinking before speaking.

"I forgot about a towel."

"I'll get one."

Marielle disappeared back into the kitchen and returned with a tea towel. She handed it to Darkly, who stood up and began wiping herself down.

"Thanks."

"What's going on?" Marielle asked, bemused.

"I need to see the other homes with children."

Marielle took Darkly to the other homes, where Wyatt found food and Darkly found bathtubs filled with water. As the threesome returned to the hotel, Darkly shared her thoughts.

"They were hiding their children in the water."

"From what?" Marielle asked.

Darkly looked at Marielle with exasperation.

"You grew up here, Marielle. You tell me."

"I've never seen this sort of thing before. My people have stayed put in Wolf Woods ten generations before I was born."

Darkly could tell Marielle wasn't lying.

Back at the hotel, the threesome settled in for a picnic of perishables that Wyatt had scavenged from the homes and washed it down with the homemade brew Darkly had the sense to bring back with them.

There were a couple hours of light left, and Darkly knew she had one other theory to test. She instructed Marielle to rest and for Wyatt to watch out the window for any movement anywhere in town or on the hills around the town and report anything he saw when Darkly got back.

"I'll be back before dark."

Darkly walked down to the river and looked across into the forest on the other side of the water.

"Here we go again."

Darkly took off her boots and socks, rolled up her jeans, and trudged out into the middle of the ford. Then, she turned south into the river and walked down the pebble slope until she was in water up to her thighs. Her jeans were wet. It didn't matter. Darkly had a crazy idea about last night. She had to test it. With Wyatt's words before his mind erasure about not singing at the forefront of her thoughts, Darkly began to do just what he had advised her against. She sang.

At first, Darkly began softly. In the great tradition of Rex Harrison, she spoke the words of a Britany Spears song. But as her courage gained strength, so did her voice become more musical. She moved on to the The Rolling Stones and Nirvana. After a while she was belting out classic pop and rock at the top of her lungs and splashing through the water. It was a great release. But, she never took her eyes off the forest.

Until another sound overpowered her voice. It was the sound of a drum. No, clanging, was more like it. A spoon against a pot. She looked behind her to see the distant figure of Wyatt hanging out of the window banging on a drain spout with what looked like the leg of a chair.

Her eyes moved down, as the hair all over her body became electrified. There, standing on the bank she had walked out into the river from, she saw what the Mounties who spent too much time in the woods spoke among themselves about with knowing glances. It was a sasquatch. This was no Harry And The Hendersons breed. It was about ten feet and covered in reddish brown hair. It's blood-shot eyes were boring into Darkly, and its head and neck were twitching in erratic fashion. It was desperate to get to Darkly, but wouldn't dare go into the water. Instead, it just reached its jaw out in Darkly's direction and gnashed its yellowed teeth.

Darkly had never been so afraid. She was so scared that she forgot to draw her gun.

CHAPTER SIX

The creature paced along the river's bank, growing more agitated by the water that separated it from Darkly. It repeatedly turned away from the river, then took a couple of giant strides, as though it intended to brave its greatest fear. But, in the end, it stood no closer to Darkly, malcontent and slobbering and grunting. Its face was disturbingly human. What was behind the eyes was disturbingly not.

Darkly remembered her gun and drew it. But, should she shoot? Did bullets have any effect on something so tall and wide? Or what if it just made the beast angrier and gave it the reason it needed to finally conquer its fear?

But the shot became a moot point, when two wolves suddenly leapt from the bushes at the creature, one latching on to an arm, and the other biting into a leg. The sasquatch howled in pain and punched one of the wolves in the skull. It fell onto its back and whimpered, while the other wolf that swung in mid-air from the beast's bough-like arm, went flying into the water, splashing Darkly.

Both wolves recovered and leapt at the legendary monster again. This time, one of the canines bit at the animal-man's crotch, while the other went for the neck. But, the beast still did not topple. It's anger elevated, the sasquatch reached down and wrapped one set of fingers around the wolf's neck and squeezed until the jaws opened up. He then threw it twenty feet through the air. The wolf landed on a stone wall. Darkly heard bones break, and the wolf did not get back up.

Suddenly, a raven swept down from the sky, appearing from nowhere. Well, to be honest, Darkly's attention wasn't exactly on the clouds. It grazed the top of the sasquatch's head, as the creature wrapped both of its arms around the remaining wolf, ready to crush its ribcage.

The bird distracted the sasquatch enough, that when the wolf sunk its teeth deeper into the creature's neck, it stumbled and slipped on the slick stones at the edge of the water. In it went, tumbling into the river.

The wolf let go, and Darkly watched as the sasquatch clamored out of the water like it had been bathing in acid and scurried away, screaming, sometimes on all fours, sometimes on two legs.

As Darkly watched the raven fly away, the two wolves that presumably saved her life lay on the riverbank. One was panting, its body half in and half out of the river. The other was deathly still.

Wyatt followed Darkly back to the hotel, carrying the naked and wounded Marielle. This girl never gets a break, thought Darkly. She had tried to kill her when they first met, and now she had saved Darkly's skin. She guessed they were really even now. Darkly noticed she was humming. In fact, she had never stopped from the moment the attack began. Like a broken record, she was compelled to repeat a few chords over and over. She had been under a spell. She had to get a handle on this.

Marielle was half-conscious when Darkly tucked her into bed. Her eyes opened, as a coughing fit overcame her. Blood sprayed from her mouth onto the pillow under her head.

"There's internal bleeding, and her back's broken. But, it wasn't a silver bullet," Darkly said to Wyatt, who sat at the end of the bed on a stool.

"She fought well," he concluded.

There was genuine concern in Wyatt's voice.

"You both did," replied Darkly. "I need you to watch her, bring her food."

"You're leaving?"

"Just for a couple of days. I will be back."

Marielle coughed again. More fresh blood.

"My baby. Is it okay?"

Darkly responded to Marielle's mumbled plea not knowing whether she spoke the truth or not.

"You'll be fine. The baby will be fine *if* you rest now. I have to talk to a friend. Someone who can help us and give me some answers."

Darkly stroked Marielle's hair and kissed her forehead.

"Sleep now. When you wake up, I'll already be back. And then we'll get out of here together."

"I need to find the father," Marielle whispered and drifted off into a place where pain was tempered by a different reality.

"Okay."

That sounded like an impossible request to Darkly. Yet, on second thought, she guessed that if one followed the bodies, the father would turn up.

Darkly looked around the room. There were enough supplies to keep Marielle and Wyatt fed for a couple of days. Maybe three. She left Marielle's side and reached out for Wyatt's hand. He took it unquestioningly, like a child. Darkly hoped his true nature remained submerged at least until she could get Marielle and herself to safety. She still hadn't decided fully if she was going to kill him or not.

"I am giving you my word as a Mountie. I'm coming back for you. Do you believe me?"

Wyatt nodded *yes.*

"Don't go outside," were Darkly's parting words.

Darkly had thought about waiting until morning and then decided there had been enough waiting. Perhaps the creature could see better in the dark than her. In fact, after the cave, she was certain of it. Surely she had speed on her side with the jeep.

Her worry was unfounded. Her journey to the main highway in the open-top jeep was entirely uneventful. For now, the beast was spooked, and she had a nine-hour drive ahead of her that she hoped would remain surprisingly banal. She'd find her way to the home of Ennis McWhorter, RCMP Retired, in time for breakfast.

Luckily for Darkly, there was a full can of gas in the back of the jeep that got her to a station along the Trans-Canada Highway. Filled up with coffee and fuel, she pushed through to the outskirts of Kamloops and pulled down the gravel driveway of her father's best friend's home as dawn was breaking.

Ennis's grandfather was a Scotsman who fought in the Great War. After the horrors of the trenches, he sought out the most remote place on earth he could find for the *peace that only nature can afford one*, as he liked to say. In British Columbia, he met a First Nations woman, whom he hired as a housekeeper and who stayed for marriage.

Ennis's native heritage shaped his attitude and actions through-out his years as an RCMP constable. He also inherited his long white hair from his grandmother's side of the family. His relation-ships with First Nations communities was the reason for Darkly's visit.

Her host had seen Darkly grow up and become a constable in her own right. So, when she showed up at his door, it was as though he was greeting his own daughter. Having never married or had children, Darkly was the closest thing to a daughter that Ennis, in fact, had. Ennis fed Darkly and sent her to bed with the promise to wake her up by lunchtime. He did just that by chopping wood outside her window midday.

A rejuvenating shower later, and Darkly was sitting across from Ennis on his back porch, drinking the universal elixir of cold beer.

"Well, are you going to tell me what you're doing here?" Ennis asked.

"I can't go into too much detail," Darkly said sheepishly.

"Ah. Undercover mission. I see."

Darkly smiled and took a swig of beer.

"I've got a really weird question to ask you."

Ennis leaned forward.

"Well, now you've got me intrigued."

"Did you and dad ever see giant men in the northern forests?" Darkly asked bluntly.

"Giants?"

There was no hint of ridicule in Ennis's voice.

"Hairy giants. About ten feet tall."

Ennis leaned back and thought about it.

"I said it was a weird question," Darkly said apologetically.

"It's not that weird."

Ennis got up.

"Come with me."

Ennis led Darkly off the porch and to a separate building from the house. Inside, Ennis stored his snowmobile, snow plow, and other winter essentials. He led Darkly to the back of the garage and a locked door. Ennis unlocked it and flicked a switch on the interior wall. Fluorescent lights blinked to life.

"After you," said Ennis.

Darkly stepped inside the back room. It was a bit like a museum. There were glass cases on tables that lined the perimeter of the room. Above those, on the walls, were maps of North America and photographs. Darkly's adoptive father was in more than a few of them. One photo, in particular, caught her eye. Her dad, William

Schilling, and Ennis were knelt next to a set of large footprints in mud outside a barn door.

"That was a hoax."

Ennis's words took Darkly by surprise.

"This room is a shrine to my career and your dad's. Some of the more interesting cases. This photo was taken in southern Alberta. A rancher kept losing cattle at night. Slaughtered in the fields they stood. The rancher was a city kid who inherited the ranch when his father passed away at a fairly young age. The neighbor wanted to buy the land. When the kid wouldn't sell, the neighbor tried to scare him off it."

"So, no hairy giant," said Darkly.

"No hairy giant," confirmed Ennis.

Ennis walked over to a case and opened the glass lid, lifted out a small wooden carving and handed it to Darkly. It was the figure of a person carved into the wood, like a totem.

"I had a lab carbon date it. The wood was cut about one hundred years ago."

The face of the carving looked very familiar to Darkly. She pulled the silver beads, the ones that had been inside Wyatt's head, out of her jeans pocket, careful not to touch them with her bare skin. She grasped the sinew that connected the beads instead. The mask one of the beads and the face on the carving were so similar, it was not likely to be a coincidence.

"Where did you get that?" Ennis asked, his interest further piqued.

Darkly was silent.

"Right. Top secret mission. May I?"

Ennis held out his open palm, and Darkly dropped the beads into it. Ennis rubbed his fingers over the beads.

"Do you know what these are?" Ennis asked.

Darkly knew very well what they had been used for recently, but not what use they were normally meant for.

"Something of a shaman's?" she guessed.

"Well, yes," said Ennis, "it would have belonged to a shaman."

Ennis held the bead up with the mask.

"This is sasquatch. Many First Nations people consider him a spiritual protector, who comes down from the highest parts of the mountains when the tribe is in trouble. This would have been a full necklace at one time. Silver. It was put around the necks of the sick to ward off evil. To protect from further infection, and, legend says, shapeshifters."

Ennis dropped the beads back in Darkly's hand.

"Shapeshifters?"

"Men and women who can take animal form."

"Like a bird," Darkly thought aloud.

"Yes," confirmed Ennis. "Or, say, a wolf."

This certainly got Darkly's attention. Was Ennis testing her? Did he suspect something about what Darkly was up to? He had been in the woods his whole adult life. He'd surely heard it all.

"You didn't answer my question, Ennis."

"There was a time you used to call me *Uncle* Ennis."

"You didn't answer my question, Uncle Ennis."

"Snow blindness, frostbite, dehydration, hunger, isolation. All these things play tricks with the mind. You can see things that aren't there. I once thought I saw a McDonald's drive-thru in the middle of the tundra."

"And did you ever think you saw sasquatch?" Darkly pressed.

Ennis gave in.

"Yes. I was with your dad one summer. The feds were moving a tribe off contaminated land. Relocating them. The tribe had seen a generational spike in leukemia, which was associated with chemical deposits left behind during a local strip-mining operation. A settlement resulted in monetary compensation and new homes in a safer area. Only, the elderly people didn't want to move. They said the spirits of their ancestors lived in the surrounding woods.

And these ancestors would become angry if we carried on with the removal of the tribe."

Ennis took a break in the story and walked over to another case. He removed a plaster cast of an immense footprint and placed it on top of the case for Darkly to inspect closely.

"Your dad and I were sleeping in a trailer the mining operation had left behind. We found these prints one morning. They circled the trailer. That was night one. Night two, we woke to the whole trailer rocking back and forth."

"Did you go outside?"

Darkly was sucked in.

"Yes. We ran out with guns drawn and shone our flashlights into the trees. The night was pitch black. Your dad's beam caught the reflection of eyes. Eyes that were well above our heads and looking down at us. I caught a glimpse of a face. It was no bear. Then we heard the thing stomp away, breaking trees as it left to make sure we were aware of its power."

"Did you have any more problems?"

"We forcibly removed the last hold-outs from their homes the next day and torched the houses, so they couldn't return. I still remember the looks in those people's eyes. Not mine or your dad's finest hour, that's for sure."

"You saved their lives. That's something," Darkly offered.

"More than a few of the elders died soon after the relocation. The stress of being forced out of the only home they had ever known got to them before any disease could."

"Was that the only time you think you saw the…"

"Sasquatch? Yes. Your dad and I never reported that bit. But, there's something else. Something I never told even your father."

Darkly knew this was going to be important. She was getting goosebumps already.

"My grandmother was 100% First Nations. She would teach me the words of the Haida. Her people called the man of the woods the Gagiit. And it was something to be feared. But it was also a creature that could be controlled."

"Controlled? For what purpose?" Darkly needed to know.

"My grandmother said the Gagiit could be called through song. Not all, but some of my grandmother's people believed it would come out of the woods to attack the enemy of the Haida, as they also believed the Gagiit were their ancestors who remembered familial bonds."

Okay. Now, Ennis was in familiar territory. Darkly had heard this before.

"Like grandparents?"

"Many times removed. During times of extreme famine in winter, when people turned to cannibalism to survive, the cannibal would become almost immortal from the life he had eaten. But, it would also transform the eater into the primitive version of man."

"This is helpful, Uncle Ennis. Is there anything else you can remember your grandmother saying?"

"Only that they avoid water at all costs. They never bathe. Water is the conduit of life, and they are something not quite alive. So, the stench when they are around is the mother of all skunk attacks."

Ennis drifted off into the land of reminiscence.

"In the water I drink, bathe, baptize and hide. The Lord God will save me from being eaten alive. My grandmother would recite that poem to me when she wanted me to take a bath."

Ennis smiled. He was imagining his grandmother's face for the first time in a long time.

"Did she ever say how you kill it?" Darkly scattered the memory.

Ennis looked deeply into Darkly's eyes and did not answer for a couple of minutes. When he did answer, it was with a rather poetic response.

"Like I said, some see it as the protector. A creature of the light. Divine even. In that case, how do you kill the divine?"

"You don't," Darkly answered the rhetorical question.

"Others see the sasquatch as something born in the darkest moments experienced by the human soul and tied to this world through a tenuous strand of descendants. Maybe when the descendants are gone, the creature disappears back into the woods, never to be called out of hiding again."

Darkly could tell Ennis was chomping at the bit to ask her about the last couple of weeks. But, to his credit, he didn't pry. Darkly ate again and rested again. She would leave at nightfall. After all that she had spoken with Ennis about, she was growing very concerned about Marielle's condition and safety.

Ennis packed Darkly's jeep with supplies, including a couple plastic containers of gasoline, two big tins of bison jerky, and a 48-pack of bottled water. He then hugged his surrogate daughter and offered his help.

"Darkly, do you need me to come with you? I'm happy to come out of retirement for one more mission."

Darkly kissed Ennis on the cheek.

"Don't worry about me. I'm not alone."

After watching Darkly drive off, Ennis went back into his house and called Darkly's father, William.

As she pulled onto the highway, Darkly wondered if the sasquatch was alone, or if there were many of the old Indian's ancestors circling the hotel at this very moment. The wind blew through Darkly's hair, and she felt a great sense of purpose. If she could not yet face the monster within, the one without would do. She understood now that to hold the beast at bay, she must take on the old Indian. Once Marielle was well enough to travel, she would say goodbye to Wolf Woods for good. Maybe she should take a page from her father and Ennis's book and burn the godforsaken place to the ground.

Sunrise was a couple of hours away when Darkly made the turn off the highway onto the final few miles stretch into Wolf Woods.

She had filled up with gas two hours before, so she could make the final run with full confidence. But, she still felt vulnerable in the open jeep. She had good reason to feel that way.

Darkly felt unnerved as she drove the incline up to the point that looked out over the town and prayed silently that the turn-off to the right that led down to the ford in the Moon River was just seconds away.

All of sudden, something swooped down in front of Darkly's face, brushing her cheek. Startled, she swerved the jeep to the left, driving off the edge of the dirt road, but managed to regain control of the vehicle and return to the road. Was it a bat?

Darkly gunned the engine. She was creeped out now and was making a run for it. She was convinced the creature was watching her from the forest. The headlights picked up the turn in the road ahead. At that moment, black claws descended from the sky, dive bombing the jeep. Darkly screamed and slammed on the brakes, as a raven came to a landing on the top edge of the windshield.

Darkly sat there not breathing as the raven gave out a low croak. "Holy fuck."

The bird tilted its head, then looked into Darkly's eyes, then looked behind her. It took off, croaking repeatedly. Darkly looked behind her, following the raven's flight. The wings disappeared into the darkness. She took a moment to collect herself and breathe. She instinctually hummed a tune from her childhood to calm her nerves. Something about teddy bears going out into the woods to enjoy a picnic. It was quiet. Except for the occasional pinging of the jeep's engine and the crickets. Then there was her breathing. It was a lot heavier and louder than she realized.

Only, the breathing wasn't coming from her. It was behind her and growing louder. Darkly peered into the darkness where the raven's wings had disappeared. The darkness seemed to be moving. Coming closer. Then it emerged. The face of the creature. The whites of its eyes and teeth. The slobbering. The stench. It was almost inside the jeep. The humming had been a bad idea.

Darkly hit the gas, and the jeep leapt forward and sputtered out. In her terror, she had forgotten to put the jeep into first gear. She slammed her left foot down on the clutch, shifted into gear and turned the engine. The jeep raced forward just as the beast leapt onto the back of the jeep. The sasquatch, the cannibal, was directly behind Darkly, ready to rip her head off.

Darkly summoned all of her resolve and drove forward, swerving the jeep violently from left to right, forcing the sasquatch to grab hold of Darkly's seat. She could feel its god-awful, blood-soaked breath on her cheek. It was no use. This was the end.

But, then, a howl of pain from the thing. Darkly looked in the rearview mirror and saw the raven bouncing off the creature's head, clawing at its face, puncturing its eyes. It was forced to leap up, and Darkly seized her chance. She turned the vehicle sharply to the right and dove down the hill toward the crossing in the river. The beast went flying, falling out of the jeep. Darkly was in the clear. Or so she thought.

The monster landed on its feet and swatted at the bird with one fist, hitting its body as a bat to ball. The bird was knocked into the forest with such ferocity, Darkly thought she could hear its bones breaking. It couldn't be anything else but dead.

Then the sasquatch began running again. Darkly had made it furious.

CHAPTER SEVEN

Maggie never imagined herself in the arms of a Mohawk warrior. But neither had she imagined herself a widow in a war with her own father's people. The people who had killed her husband and occupied her land. Americans. And now she served them food and ale as a barmaid at the Angel Inn.

The landlord had taken pity on her and given her a cot in the cellar among the casks. He'd also taken in an Indian with a bounty on his head. Raton, he was called. It was not his given name, but it was all the landlord could manage in the translation of a name he couldn't spell. And it sounded remotely French. It stuck and was shortened to Rat during the occasional condemnation from employer to employee.

Raton watched Maggie. He watched her while he was cooking the soup. He watched her while he was washing the dishes. He watched her while she was on her knees scrubbing the floor. She could feel his eyes touching her.

He scared Maggie at first. Twice the size of her, with one eye scarred from when a British soldier had tried to pluck it out. Raton cut out the man's heart and disappeared into the wilderness before they could hang him. Lieutenant Fitzgibbon sent Mohawk warriors with no love loss for Raton after him. He slit both of their throats and found sanctuary in American-occupied territory.

To say the Mohawk was a hard man was an understatement. As a boy, he had witnessed his father forced to watch, as his mother was raped multiple times by French trappers. At the end of the long night, the trappers hanged Raton's parents and enslaved the boy as a mule. For eight years, he lugged beaver and muskrat pelts, until at age fifteen, he found his moment for revenge. After a night of drinking, Raton tied the trappers up in their sleep and, one by one, cut their cocks off and shoved them in their screaming mouths. Then he gutted each one of them like a salmon, and they bled to death. Raton was free, yet never free of the pain of his past.

When he looked at Maggie, he saw a kindred spirit. Everything she had hoped and planned for had been reduced to enduring the gropes of slobbering boys fighting a war that none of them could recite the reasons for the start of hostilities.

Maggie had gone from avoiding Raton's gaze at all times to stealing a look when she thought Raton was not aware to catching her breath and wiping sweat from her upper lip when he brushed against her in the kitchen. Until one night, after the last pissed American soldier had been pushed out the door to take his chances with snipers and locals prostituting themselves, Maggie made her way down to the cot amid the wine and beer.

She undid her hair and set to brushing out the tangles. It was when she put the brush down on the top of a cask, that Raton stepped out of the shadows. Maggie reacted as she would be expected to. She backed herself into a barrel, as her eyes darted to the cellar steps, planning her escape.

But, then, Raton reached his hand out for Maggie's. It rested there, unshaking on thin air, with Maggie's eyes fixed on Raton's.

To her own surprise, she accepted it. She pulled his hand to her waist, and then turned to brace herself against a barrel of port. She felt Raton's rough hands run themselves up her legs and lift her petticoat, and she gave herself to him.

Even more of a surprise was it to Maggie when she discovered she loved Raton. But as strong as her love was for her kindred spirit, the Mohawk, stronger was her hatred for the men who had struck down her husband. The most Raton could hope for was that the war would last years rather than months. For, the inevitable silencing of muskets to come would end their relationship. War tolerates strange bedfellows. Peace does not. But, Maggie would come to ask more of Raton before it was all over.

It was during the serving of supper at the Angel Inn, when Maggie's opportunity for revenge revealed itself. She had placed the legs of turkey down in front of the captain and the beautiful corporal sitting across from him – a young man for whom the officer carried a decidedly un-fatherly affection – when the captain said too much. With his fingertips almost touching the boy's, the captain mentioned that the undermanned and underprepared British Lieutenant Fitzgibbon was about to receive the surprise of a bayonet up the backside.

It was that night, after making love, that Maggie asked Raton to help her find her way to the people who would burn him alive if they caught him. And because he loved her, he did not hesitate with his answer.

But, to the captain with the loose lips, Maggie's interest in what he had to say had not gone unnoticed. Pubs had been the preferred hangout of spies since Marlowe's day. And the captain knew that women made the best spies.

It was just before dawn, when Maggie and Raton took provisions from the larder, said goodbye to the Angel Inn, and walked quietly from house to house until reaching the edge of town. It was at the end of town, where the road turned toward Queenston Heights, that the captain's men were waiting for Maggie.

It all happened so fast. No warnings were given; no questions were asked. A shot ran out. Standing fifty feet in front of Maggie in the pale blue of pre-dawn and the smoke of musket fire, were two men. When she turned to Raton, she realized he was not standing at all.

As the men slowly approached, Maggie knelt next to her lover. The musket ball had caught him in the neck. His carotid artery was severed, but Raton had enough strength left to remove a knife and slide it into Maggie's hand. By the time she lifted her lips from Raton's, he was gone, and she was being hoisted to her feet.

Maggie now possessed the rage of two loves lost. She turned and plunged the knife she was hiding into the captain's gut, and ran.

She heard the captain scream through his pain, "Shoot her!"

The beautiful corporal fumbled with his loaded musket at first, but successfully fired.

Maggie felt the searing pain in her side, but the adrenaline coursing through her body kept her going. She ran. No soldier could stop her now.

It was mid-morning when Maggie reached the Secord house. She knew, as she collapsed onto the porch, and Laura Secord came rushing to her side, that she had lost too much of her blood to recover. There was only one rest that could cure her.

But before that, she would ask the loyalist Secord to fulfill what she would now be unable to complete.

Leaving Maggie's burial to her husband, whose war wounds were too severe to undertake any journey, Laura Secord set off for DeCou House, some twenty miles away. And as the American contingent approached her home, Laura knew she could not hope to beat the US soldiers on horseback. She repeated the name DeCou to herself over and over as she ran through the woods that surrounded her homestead.

With the cavalry horses' hooves felt in the ground below her, Laura collapsed to all fours. The name DeCou swam laps through her head until even that repetition gave way to the mind of the wolf. But the wolf knew she was being chased. And she knew where she was going. She had been there before. This time, she brought information that could change the tide of the war.

⊨┼┼⊨

Like Laura Secord, Darkly knew what was chasing her, ready to strike her down. Something big that shook the ground, and only yards behind. Unlike Laura, as much as she wanted to at that very moment, there was no spontaneous metamorphosis onto all fours. Darkly had only the steel chassis and four wheels below her. Looking behind her at the gaining creature, Darkly also knew they would not be enough.

The headlights reflected off the ripples in the river and wet stones ahead. If she could get to the water, then she'd be safe for a time. It was then she saw the figure standing in the middle of the ford.

So, it was true, she thought, there is more than one. And this one had overcome its fears. She had no choice but to run it down. She suspected it would be like hitting a tree. At least the end would be quick.

The jeep left the bank and hit the slick rocks at over fifty miles per hour. It was only a split second she had to determine that the figure in front of her was not a corruption of nature, but a simple man.

Darkly swerved the jeep at the last possible millisecond and plummeted into deeper water, causing a wave to reach up over the windshield and wash her out of the jeep. The figure standing in the river was no sasquatch. It was Buck.

Darkly spluttered to her feet and watched as Sheriff Buck raised the biggest shotgun she'd ever seen and empty its barrel into all that hair and muscle. The barrel of the firearm opened up at the end into what looked like a trumpet. It was the kind of gun that brought down big game in Africa. This particular North American game also succumbed to its power.

"We need to get inside before the rest come," Buck said to Darkly with no betrayal of fear.

"There's more?" Darkly asked.

"A legion of them. You shouldn't have come back."

Buck walked to the bank, and Darkly followed. The sky was turning the palest of blue.

"I'm in the hotel."

"Good. We'll be able to see the whole town from there."

"I'm not alone."

Buck stopped and grabbed Darkly's arm.

"You've brought outsiders to Wolf Woods? Knowing all you know, you would put more people in danger?"

"Hey, I came back to help you," Darkly said defiantly.

Buck shone a flashlight in Darkly's face. He immediately noticed her neck.

"What have you done?"

"Don't worry, sheriff. I appear to be cured."

Darkly stormed past him onto the bank. As she did, a whooping sound shot out of the woods behind them. It was a chorus of whoops. Many voices. Buck leapt up the bank to join Darkly, grabbed her arm, and they both ran for the hotel.

Once inside the hotel, Buck hit the light switch. Nothing.

"The generator's burned out," Buck informed Darkly.

"I know."

Buck bolted the front door and pointed his flashlight at the lobby sofas.

"We need to barricade the door."

Buck and Darkly slid one heavy antique sofa across the floor and slammed it up against the front door.

"You think that will stop them?" Darkly asked.

"What do you think?" he retorted. "Who's here with you?"

"Marielle," Darkly answered. "She came back."

"Damn. I told that girl never to return."

"She was injured."

Buck shook his head at Darkly's words.

"Who else?"

"Just one other."

Buck and Darkly stood in silence for a moment. Realization dawned on Buck's face.

"Wyatt," Buck said through clenched teeth and made a beeline for the staircase.

Darkly tried to grab him, but he shook her off.

"He's changed, Buck. You have to listen to me."

Buck leapt two stairs at a time, and Darkly raced after him. But, he made it to her room before her and managed to kick it in on the first try. The frame splintered, and Darkly heard Marielle scream, as Buck flung himself inside the room.

Darkly was only a second behind him.

There, on the bed, was Wyatt on his back, and Marielle straddling him. Candles placed every few feet around the room illuminated the lovers. Marielle scrambled off Wyatt and pulled a sheet around her naked body. But not before Darkly noticed the small bulge. Could that be a baby bump? This quickly?

Buck reached for Wyatt's hair, as his brother tried to cover his large erection. Buck dragged him out of bed and pressed him face-first into the wall. The sheriff then pulled his revolver out and pressed the barrel to Wyatt's forehead.

"I – I – I," Wyatt stuttered.

"Well? Death, destruction, exile. You've condemned us all. It must be everything you've ever wanted. Tell us all how proud you are of yourself before I shoot this silver bullet through one ear and out the other."

"Buck. He's not himself," Darkly said softly.

"His wife and son just killed, and he's fucking a girl half his age. I'd say he's very much himself."

"Son?" Wyatt asked and slid down the wall to the ground.

Buck's gun didn't leave the side of his brother's head, and Wyatt began to cry. Darkly gently and slowly placed her hand on Buck's arm.

"He doesn't remember who he is."

"He's a good liar, and you've fallen for it."

"She's telling the truth," Marielle chimed in. "He's lost. In the head."

Darkly removed the shaman beads from her pocket and held them in front of Buck.

"I found him up on the overlook. Tied up. By the time we pulled these out of him, he couldn't have told you his name."

Buck looked from Wyatt to the beads and back again. He reluctantly lowered his gun and walked to the other side of the room.

"I'm the one who left him up there to die. I don't know anything about the beads."

"Why did you come back?" asked Darkly.

Buck turned away from the wall to look at Wyatt, who's head was buried in his hands.

"There was a time when he was my brother. I decided to put him out of his misery. Make it quick. Instead of eaten by those things out there."

Buck looked at his gun with what appeared to be regret that he didn't get to use it, and then holstered it.

"You got any food?" Buck asked, changing the subject.

Wyatt was dressed, but still sat on the floor, not looking at anyone. He had withdrawn into himself, no doubt trying to find what was there. Darkly, for one, hoped he never found it. Buck ate pickled cauliflower from a jar and looked Marielle up and down. She sat by the window, watching for movement outside. She felt Buck's eyes boring into her.

"Darkly said you were hurt."

"Shot. Then burned by a farmer."

Buck walked over to Marielle and pulled the curtains closer together and looked down at her stomach. Marielle pulled Darkly's jacket around herself tightly.

"I did what I was supposed to."

"And the father. Where's he?"

Marielle shrugged.

"Then you didn't do what was asked of you. You were supposed to build a family after whoring yourself out."

"Hey! That's enough."

Darkly shut Buck down and put her arm around Marielle, who looked genuinely wounded by the statement.

"What's wrong with you?" Darkly continued.

Buck looked outside. The sun was very low on the horizon.

"What happened here before now?"

The question came from Wyatt. His eyes were red, but his face was alert, and he was seeking answers.

"You don't want to know," Buck shot back.

"Yes, Buck. *We* do. What happened after you assured me it would all be okay?"

Darkly waited impatiently for Buck to answer. She also had a right to know what threats the outside world, her world, was now facing. She was technically a wolf. One that could not turn. But a wolf. Buck surely respected that. Okay, so she was back to thinking that home was the three-bedroom house she grew up in, with people in it who were only human. It was hard to feel attached to a place that her own kind had abandoned.

Buck ate a few more pickles, then began to speak at length.

"Wyatt's men had taken hostages. Shields. When I caught up to him, he had a knife to Trey's throat."

CHAPTER EIGHT

Wyatt smiled at Buck, as he dragged Trey into the church. Victoria, as wolf, growled at Wyatt, pacing back and forth in front of the entrance to the holy place. Buck could hear the shots behind him, the screaming, the wolves fighting to the death. The war for Wolf Woods was underway.

Buck leapt into town, attacking one of Wyatt's horde and killing him almost instantly in self-defense. This bold act bolstered the townsfolk. The prodigal son would not be welcomed home. Wolf Woods had chosen its alpha. Buck was with them, and they were with Buck to the end.

But there was another. Neither of Buck's or Wyatt's clan. An old man. The last of his tribe, who had been waiting in the woods for just such a time of chaos, when the wolves would turn against each other. His people had last defended their home and hunting grounds from the wolves when he was a small boy. His father and his uncles were killed, along with most of their tribe. His mother and he fled north, deeper into the woods to wait.

It was during that time he learned how to call his ancestors from even deeper in the forest and from the mountain tops.

Through dance and song, he lured them from their purgatory. The lost ones who fed their famine with the flesh of their kin. But not his flesh. He controlled them with the lullabies of past lives they almost forgot.

Now, with his army of sasquatch, the old man would finally take his revenge and rid his forest of the wolves. There would be justice for his mother and father and all those who came before them.

He had been watching, as Buck left his people. He watched as the killer brother returned to reclaim Wolf Woods, and then he waited for war to erupt. When it did just that, the old man knew how to strike fear into the already rattled wolves. His army would target their children. And they would start with the killer's own son.

Wyatt slammed the front doors of the church shut and locked them, never loosening his grip on Trey.

"Now you listen to me. My brother is not your father, boy. I am."

Trey struggled against Wyatt, who pressed the knife closer against his neck.

"Stop!" Wyatt commanded. "Think about it. Why do you think he's so opposed to you mating with my daughter?"

Trey stopped struggling.

"That got your attention, didn't it? I don't care if you fuck your sister, aunt or brother. You can fuck whoever you want. Eat whoever you want. I'm back for you. To make sure that you become the alpha. It's your birthright. But, your birthright through me, not Buck. Are you listening?"

Trey stared into Wyatt's eyes.

"Good. Now, I'm going to let you go. Don't run. If I have to kill you, I will. I have a spare. He's not much in the brain's department, but I'm sure Victoria could fuck him into shape."

Trey twitched at that. Wyatt slowly pulled the knife away and released Trey. The boy moved a few inches away, and Wyatt held his knife at the ready. It was then that the faint sound of drums found its way through the church doors. Wyatt pointed at a bend in the entranceway.

"Sit."

Trey didn't move. The drums grew louder.

"Sit," repeated Wyatt more forcefully.

Trey sat, and Wyatt took a glimpse out of a window. The color drained from his face. He ran back to Trey, grabbed the boy's arm and ran into the sanctuary.

Wyatt raced down the aisle, dragging Trey behind him. He pushed Trey up onto the altar and then began feeling the panels of the wall behind the altar. Finally, one gave way, just as the wood of the front doors shattered in an almighty crack of thunder. The whole building seemed to shake.

"Shit. Judgment day. Just my fucking luck."

Wyatt pushed Trey through the panel, followed him in, and shut the panel behind them. In the panel, at eye level, was a small grate, disguised on the outside by artwork. On the inside of this storage cupboard, the grate was the only source of illumination. A small shaft of light fed by the lightbulbs in the sanctuary fell on Wyatt's and Trey's eyes. Wyatt pulled Trey in front of him to look through the grate. The boy gasped, and Wyatt immediately covered the boy's mouth with his hand.

Trey's eyes teared up as the sound of grunting and snorting grew near to the hiding place. Then it stopped and was replaced by a slow, long inhale. Wyatt pulled Trey back into him, keeping his hand firmly planted on the teenager's mouth. They sank into the back wall of the shallow space and watched the tips of three black, leathery fingers push their way through the grate and then withdraw.

Wyatt let his hand fall away from Trey's mouth, just as a hairy fist broke through the panel and opened its hand. It wrapped itself around Trey's throat and pulled him through the panel like it was made of paper.

Wyatt tried to burrow backwards through the wall behind him, as he watched the sasquatch throw Trey onto the pews below the altar. Trey's body cracked, and he tumbled to the floor unconscious. The sasquatch turned it's not quite human face to Wyatt. It stood on the outside of the panel and simply jutted its neck into the storage space, moving its face to within a few millimeters of Wyatt's. It opened its mouth in a smile of crooked brown teeth and drool. The smile grew wider.

Then the howl came.

The sasquatch pulled its head free and spun around to face five wolves tearing down the aisle of the sanctuary. They leapt over Trey's prostrate body and tackled the sasquatch. One wolf suffered a shattered jaw from the sasquatch's punch on first contact and dragged itself whimpering behind the altar. But the four wolves remaining were enough to bring the ancient beast to its knees.

That was exactly the circumstance needed for Wyatt to turn wolf and remove himself from the equation. He left the church to find a town overrun and his son, Roland, being dragged by the hair into an alleyway, where the beast that had him began pummeling his body until it burst open. Wyatt the wolf turned in circles, losing his human mind, while screams filled the air above the town.

The attack was house-to-house. Families barricaded themselves inside their homes. Outside, those damned drums threatened to knock down walls with their booming. The wolves were on the defensive, and the old man knew he had won. But, the wolves remembered their fairytales. They hid their children in overflowing baths and turned garden hoses on the invaders. To lure them out, the old man would need to take hostages.

Lily heard the howling and screaming from her bedroom window. She watched her father's, now her sheep, run in one wave for higher ground up the fields at the edge of town. The best place in danger, she knew, was the fruit cellar at the end of the garden. She would wake Serena and take her there, until the sheriff came to report the all-clear. Whoever the sheriff ended up being.

She and her new mother would not make it to the cellar. As fast as they could run, the creatures were faster. Though, the feared death did not come. Lily and Serena were scooped up like pets and carried away. In the woods just across the Moon River, they were dropped by a fireside, where an old man danced a forgotten rhythm to ghost drums, and wolf pups huddled together.

Then, the attack was completed. The drumming ended abruptly, and the sasquatch simply sank into the mist. They disappeared.

Buck stood as man once again over the mortally wounded sasquatch in the church. It gurgled and spit up blood. It looked around at the other naked townsfolk. It was confused, alone, not comprehending death after God knows how many years of cheating it. Its eyes glazed over, and its body went limp.

Gus kneeled by Geraldine, whose mouth was bleeding and jaw dislocated. He pulled a cloth from the altar and tied her jaw to the top of her head. What a sight. She was in great pain, but her concern was with Trey's body. Buck followed her gaze to where Victoria was kissing his son's face.

Buck kneeled by Trey, who moaned.

"He's alive," Victoria said with relief.

Buck nodded.

"I'll be right back."

Buck left the church to find a quiet street. Only one man was there. Wyatt stood in the middle of the road holding his son's irreparably broken body. Drifting on the air, Buck heard the sound of crying. It was building and came from all directions to replace the drumming that had stopped. He knew what it meant.

"They're gone," Wyatt told Buck. "His heart burst. He won't heal. I need to burn his body."

Buck nodded his head, and Wyatt walked past the brother who was firmly back in charge. Buck turned to see Victoria helping Trey out of the church.

"Son," Buck said, as he approached the two.

Trey stopped Buck with his eyes. They were wounded, cold. They communicated, *we're not alright.* Buck would sit Trey down another time. Right now, Buck needed to add up the wounded and the dead. And the number of children who had been taken from their inconsolable parents.

Buck went house to house that night. It was five. Five missing children. All of them not yet thirteen. The price to get them back was going to be high. He needed to speak with Geraldine. It was time. Fate was forcing their hand. That same fate was brought on by the foul wind Wyatt road into town. He'd pay for this. Blood or no blood, Buck was ready to become a killer.

Buck returned to his office and began rifling through papers. He was throwing everything on the floor, tearing up his own office. Geraldine walked through the front door. Her face was bruised, but she had removed the Scrooge bandaging.

"What are you doing?" she mumbled.

"There was an Indian. Someone my grandfather told me about. A shaman he said could command the dead."

Geraldine put her hand on Buck's.

"Stop. Pour me a drink."

Buck continued to look through papers, but eventually dropped most of the sheets in his hand and dropped his ass into his chair to look at a black and white photograph of an old First Nations man sitting in the cell a few feet away. Buck turned the photo over to see a date written in pencil. 1932. And the words, *The last one.* He reached into a drawer and pulled out an unmarked bottle and a couple of glasses.

"Huh. Wyatt didn't drink it all yet."

Buck poured Geraldine and himself a shot of moonshine. Geraldine swallowed the spirit in one gulp and winced in pain.

"Hurts?" Buck asked.

"Yes," Geraldine responded, forcing her injured mouth to turn up in a smile. "There's too many of them. We can't win. You know that. The children are the bargain. It's over."

Buck swallowed his shot.

"Okay. But we're leaving one bastard behind."

Geraldine knew exactly who Buck was talking about.

Buck walked out into the Moon River under a bright morning sun. A loon drifted on the current a few yards away. Behind him, Geraldine, Gus, and several other brave souls had Buck's back on the town-side riverbank. Standing in the middle of the ford was the old Indian. Buck couldn't see them, but he knew who had the old man's back.

Buck stopped about six feet from the man. They nodded at one another.

"What do you want?" Buck asked the old man.

"What I have always wanted. What my ancestors wanted when you drove them off our lands. To come home."

"I can provide you with a house of your own. Food," Buck offered.

"I don't think so."

The old man smiled.

"Are the children safe?"

"Of course. I have kept them close."

With great flare, the old man flung open his long hide coat, and the five children, including Lily came running out. Splashing through the water, they ran to hide themselves behind Buck. The old man then turned in a circle, his front disappearing from Buck's view for a couple of seconds and reappearing again, with Serena holding tightly to the Indian's midriff. She ran to join Lily.

"We will need a week to prepare," Buck said with as much humility as he could muster.

"You have until the next sundown."

The old man turned and began walking to the other side of the river. He continued to speak.

"I will not take hostages the next time."

Buck and Geraldine organized the exodus from Wolf Woods speedily. Most everything would need to be left behind. The few working vehicles would carry people, not supplies. Cash from the outside world was useless here. But, plans were put in motion decades ago for just such an end times event. Disease and hunger were not reasons to send out emissaries with money. Settling colonists like Marielle and the relocating of the entire town were why the thousands of stolen dollars were now being piled onto the hood of Buck's pickup. For thousands of years, Buck's kind never got too comfortable in one place.

Buck's time as sheriff was coming to an end. For now. There would be no need for an alpha when there is no community. One of his last official duties was to divvy up the money among the families. Then the convoy would move out. The plan was to drive to the U.S. border, where some families would cross into the country to the south, and others would move east. It was certain this was the last time Buck would look many of his extended family in the eye. It was too soon. They weren't ready for this. Yet, here they found themselves, setting out to convert the world. Whenever does change happen according to schedule? And how ironic was it that the wolf who was never destined to be alpha would set such a plan in motion?

It hit Buck as he pocketed the last of the dough, that he had no clue where he was going. Buck spotted Trey and Victoria, lingering by the edge of the Moon River. Well, he had better get this over with. Trey looked away as he saw the man he had thought was his father approach, a wad of bills in his hand.

Buck split the bills up and handed the larger of the two parts to Victoria. She'd been crying.

"You're going to need this."

Trey still didn't look at Buck and let Victoria do the talking for both of them.

"We're not going to..." she trailed off, not able to finish the thought.

"You're not brother and sister. You're not even half way to that. My brother lied."

Trey turned to look at Buck.

"Well, he didn't think he lied. He's just not that good with dates. The RCMP constable. Darkly. She's your sister, Trey. I buried your mother up on the ridge. Your father was killed before you were born. I'm sorry. I did my best."

Buck had said his peace, and now it was time to deal with Wyatt. As he walked away, he heard the words he didn't think he would hear again.

"Dad."

Buck stopped, and Trey walked up to him. After a brief stand-off, father and son hugged it out. With his eyes tearing up, Buck gave a last word of advice.

"If you find yourself in trouble, with no way out of it, go to your sister. The world we're going out into belongs to her."

Buck watched from the sidelines as the convoy of trucks rolled out of town, across the ford in the Moon River, and made their way to the rural highway that would take them to the continent long Trans-Canada Highway. He watched as Trey drove his pickup truck up the hill on the other side of the river, Victoria pressed closely to him.

The last vehicle was an old Indian motorcycle. Gus pulled up next to Buck with Geraldine behind him.

"You sure you'll be okay on foot?" Gus asked Buck.

"I'll be far enough away from here by sundown." Buck addressed the old Indian he knew to be nearby, watching the drama unfold.

Geraldine tapped Gus on the shoulder and dismounted. She walked up to Buck, grabbed his face with both of her hands and kissed him tenderly on the lips.

"I'll see you soon."

She then got back on the bike without saying another word, and Gus drove off.

Buck walked into his office, sat down at his desk and poured himself a whisky.

"Here we are back where we started, brother."

The next words came from a jail cell. Wyatt sat on a cot in the holding cell, his wrists handcuffed.

"My wife's dead. One son dead, the other good as dead where he's going. Just the original family. Me and you, Buck."

"He's not your son. And we're not family anymore."

Wyatt laughed.

"I understand you need to tell yourself that. You never did like to talk about uncomfortable truths. You always put a wall up around yourself. An introvert, they call people like you."

Buck poured another shot and walked over to the cell. Wyatt met him at the bars, where Buck poured the whisky into Wyatt's mouth.

"So, where are we going? New York? Hollywood? Dallas? The world's our lamb, little brother."

"I haven't decided where I'm going yet."

Wyatt stepped back. He got the message, and perhaps for the first time in his life, he looked worried for his safety.

Buck pulled out his gun.

"If you try to turn, I'll shoot to kill."

An hour later, while Wyatt screamed in agony, Buck took one last look at Wolf Woods and the Moon River below. As the sheriff without a town made his way on foot to the highway, his brother, crucified with ropes and wood, laughed through the pain. Buck felt ashamed that he hoped the Indian would let his brother suffer, rather than feed him to the creatures right away.

Wyatt rocked back and forth, his arms wrapped around his knees. Buck's story of events had been too much for him.

"If the old man is controlling them, we should kill him," Marielle said emphatically.

Darkly gave Buck a knowing glance before answering her.

"You can't kill someone who's already dead."

CHAPTER NINE

Darkly dropped into a doze, when the almighty bang shook the building. She leapt to her feet, awake, and moved to Buck's side by the window.

"They're here," Darkly said, mustering her sense of calm.

"It's a test," Buck elaborated. "I've been watching one of the sasquatch. He just wanted to see what they are up against. How many will be needed to get through the door. See there, behind the dumpster? The attack will happen while it's still dark."

Darkly squinted, examining the shadows. Two pinpricks of red glowed back at her.

"There's no way out but going through them," Darkly said, facing the inevitable truth.

"No. We need them to get in."

Darkly, Marielle, and Wyatt stared back at Buck with incredulity. Buck then explained his reasoning.

"The town's reserves of heating oil are kept in the basement of the hotel. There's enough barrels to set the whole building alight. If we can kill even a few of them, our chances of getting away rise considerably."

Darkly processed the information. There were some holes in the plan.

"How do we kill them without killing ourselves? If we shoot one of the barrels, the rest will go up with it. That means one of us is going to be awfully close to the inferno."

Darkly looked at the cowering Wyatt. Was Buck planning to sacrifice his brother? Talk him into some act of repentance to save them? Buck could see where Darkly's mind was wandering. He brought a stop to the wander.

"We just need to light a few fires."

Darkly immediately followed the logic.

"We raise the temperature until the fuel becomes unstable. That's got to be pretty hot. Some fairly big fires," warned Darkly.

"There's a lot of old curtains. A set in each room. They must burn easily," Marielle weighed in.

Buck shone his flashlight on the rusting barrels that lined the basement of the hotel in rows. It looked like a scene from a horror movie. A cavern full of eggs containing gelatinous monsters about to erupt from their metal cocoons. He had curtains draped around his neck. So did Darkly, Marielle and Wyatt. Darkly immediately tied a long panel of material around a barrel. She wiped her fingertip along the top of the barrel, picking up oil residue that had seeped through the rusting lid. She smelled her finger. This wouldn't take long, she thought.

"This will do for a starter, but we need a fuel source that will burn longer."

It was Marielle who answered Darkly. She pointed to the other end of the basement, enshrined in darkness.

"The storage closet down there has wooden chairs. Enough for a hundred people or more. My uncle said they used to throw parties in the hotel. There were a lot more people then."

Darkly walked along the basement wall, shining her own flashlight into the dark. Above her in the wall, were ground level windows, whose sills were at Darkly's eye level. She looked outside. Nothing moved. But, she could make out the faint sound of a far off drum. She knew it would grow louder.

The basement room was almost the length of the building, and Darkly, thanks to experience, pulled her gun from her belt and pointed it into the darkness. She swallowed. Her mouth was dry. She could make out the door to the closet. It was ajar. Okay, she thought, that's not unusual. Behind her, she heard the shifting of barrels.

Darkly reached the open closet door and shone her light inside. She saw the piles of dusty wooden folding chairs. She slid her gun back under her belt and reached for a chair. That's when it hit her. Her mouth went numb. Then she felt her tongue swell up like a balloon, that was then popped by the points of a thousand needles bearing down on Darkly. She wasn't alone. Whoever was very near to her, they or it had killed many times. It was unlike anything she had felt before in her life. She ran.

Darkly made it only a few feet, when she saw a chair fly by her head and shatter on the ground in front of her.

"They're inside!" Darkly yelled.

Darkly dove for the first row of fuel barrels and scampered through the maze, ducking down to hide behind one of the barrels. She heard the loping of heavy feet to her side, as they passed by her, moving forward toward Buck, Wyatt, and Marielle. She poked her head above the top of the barrel to get a look. She shone her light and hit the back of the biggest thing she'd ever seen. At least twelve feet, the sasquatch was the width of a kitchen table and the color of silver gray.

The creature stopped moving, sensing the light on its back. It turned to look into the beam. The mouth and eyes were stained with blood. In its terrible face, Darkly made out muscles contorted in decades, or was it centuries, of torment? There was no pity, no curiosity. Just ferocious hunger. It swatted a barrel to its right. The drum launched into the air and crashed down onto other barrels, spilling the contents and drenching the basement with the stinging aroma of gasoline.

The gray sasquatch made a beeline for Darkly, kicking barrels out of its path like footballs.

"Keep the light on its head!"

It was Buck's voice that broke through her terror, when the monster was almost upon her. A shot rang out, and the sasquatch jerked its shoulder in pain. It looked behind it for a split second and then continued barreling down on Darkly. Another shot, and the beast threw back its head and screeched in agony. A third shot, and this ancient nightmare fell to its knees and face first onto the floor at Darkly's feet.

Darkly ran past the dead creature. Do they stay dead, she wondered again? Or were they like werewolves? She wasn't sticking around to find out. Marielle had one of the street-level windows open. Wyatt provided her with a lift, and she dived outside.

"Come on," Buck said to Darkly.

He offered Darkly a lift to join Marielle. She looked behind her at the flooded basement.

"Taking a chance firing with all this fuel, weren't you?"

"You're right, Darkly. I should have let it eat you. It would have given the rest of us more of a head start."

Darkly emerged out of the basement and looked around her. Nothing was approaching her and Marielle. Yet. But the drums were persistent. She reached down and helped pull Wyatt out, and then Buck.

"Behind the dumpster," Buck whispered.

The foursome dashed across the alley.

"We need to get to the river and swim for it. It's our only chance."

Darkly cut Buck off and shoved him to the side. She drew her gun and fired, hitting a sasquatch in the eye. The upper half of its body slumped over the sill of the hotel window from which it was crawling.

"One shot to your three," Darkly bragged to Buck.

"How come we never heard them get in?" Marielle asked, her eyes darting all around her.

"They're hunters," Darkly answered. "Silence is their best weapon."

They then watched in horror, as long hairy arms grabbed the sasquatch body and pull it back into the basement. Darkly gave Buck a look, and he nodded in response.

"On the count of three, we run for the river," Buck said, as he poked his head around the dumpster.

"It's clear. One. Two. Three."

The four jumped out from behind their hiding place and ran down the alley. When they had cleared the alleyway, Darkly stopped, turned and aimed at one of the basement windows.

"Get down on the ground," she yelled.

Darkly fired several rounds, and a second later was blown backwards, as the fuel in the hotel basement ignited. Glass and brick showered the alley, and the shock wave took Darkly's breath away. The next thing she knew, Wyatt was helping her to her feet, and the four were running again. Darkly felt the heat of the successive explosions on her back. She could no longer hear the drums, but she could hear the howls of animals being burned alive.

Darkly, Buck, Marielle, and Wyatt made it to the river without further incident. The diversion had worked. They ran into the ford and immediately made for deeper water. Darkly allowed herself to be carried away by the current. As the escapees entered the maelstrom of the first round of rapids rounding the bend in the crescent of the Moon River, Darkly looked up at the look-out point where her father had parked their RV when she was a young girl. She made out the small silhouette of a man. She assumed it was the old Indian. He watched as the hotel fire spread, and the whole town went up in flames.

Darkly spotted Marielle's head bobbing up ahead of her. She fought the white caps of the rapids to make her way to the pregnant woman, who was clearly losing the battle to keep her head above water. Marielle's head went under again when Darkly was only a foot away. It popped up an instant later as Marielle the wolf. She snapped her jaws at Darkly, who inhaled a mouthful of water and was slammed against a rock outcrop. Marielle joined the other two wolves swimming for shore. Darkly was on her own, being carried down river at a pace she couldn't fight. She was losing consciousness.

The next thing Darkly experienced was a slap to her face. Then another. Her droopy eyelids opened. A bright light was shining in her eyes. She turned her head to the side and retched. She put a hand up to block the light.

"Sorry."

It was Ennis McWhorter's voice.

"Ennis?" Darkly coughed out.

Ennis shone his flashlight on his own face.

"In the flesh. I'm afraid I followed you. I've been watching from the look-out above town. You want to tell me what's going on?"

Darkly looked around her. She was on shore, her feet still in the water. About a mile away, she could see the conflagration that used to be Wolf Woods.

"There were three other people."

"I know. I saw them enter the river with you. I'm sorry. I lost track of them. Just encountered a pack of wolves on the way down to you."

Ennis removed his rifle from his shoulder and helped Darkly sit up.

"I surprised one of them. I had to shoot. You okay to walk? My truck's about a two-hour hike from here. Your father wants you to come home, Darkly."

"You shot one of them?"

Darkly was on her feet now.

"Where?"

"Right over..."

Ennis turned to look over his shoulder and stopped speaking. Darkly looked around him to see Wyatt's naked body lying in the fetal position about ten yards away.

The hike back to Ennis's car took all night. Ennis carried Wyatt over his shoulders like a sack of flour. Ennis was a big man. It wasn't a chore. Relieved and confounded to see that Darkly was right, and that Wyatt was merely unconscious, his wounds healing rapidly on their own, Ennis did not complain. At Darkly's request, he also didn't ask any questions, when she insisted they travel ten miles out of their way in a roundabout approach to Ennis's truck. Darkly didn't disappoint Ennis when she unburdened herself, revealing the unabridged account of events she had denied Ennis two days before.

When Wyatt awoke in Ennis's home, Darkly was there to explain why it was best for him to remain with Ennis while she returned to Toronto. Despite all the terrible things he used to be, Darkly found herself secretly wishing she could take Wyatt with her. He was that connection to all that had happened to her over the past two weeks. He was proof that it had all been real. My God, she thought. Only two weeks. Then return to civilization she did.

CHAPTER TEN

William was there to meet Darkly's plane. She threw herself into his arms. It felt like years since she last felt his touch. She pulled away and considered his eyes. There was love in them, but also the other thing she was looking for. Recognition.

"You knew," she said.

"Come on. Let's go have a drink."

William took his daughter to his old watering hole from when he was a constable. The English pub was covered with law enforcement badges from across the globe and the crests of provinces, states and far-off lands, where kangaroos and flightless birds found their way onto official emblems.

Darkly didn't realize how famished she was. She tore into her bloody steak and sopped up the blood with a piece of toasted bread.

"You used to like your meat well-done," Darkly's father observed.

Darkly looked at the bread. It's true. Things had changed. She had changed. She could feel it. William's eyes lingered over the spot where her silver necklace used to lie. Darkly used her napkin to pull the silver shaman beads from her pocket and put them down on the table in front of her father.

"You know what those are, don't you?"

There was only the slight tone of accusation in Darkly's voice. She was not on the attack. She just wanted answers.

"Yes," William answered.

"Uncle Ennis told me silver is used to ward off shape-shifters. Like me."

William swallowed the last of his beer.

"I'll get us two more. I'll call your mother and let her know we'll be late."

While William stood at the bar and placed his call, Darkly absent-mindedly ran the beads through her fingers and dropped them. If her eyes couldn't see, she would have sworn her hand had burst into flames. She picked the beads up again with the napkin and dropped them into the glass of water sitting untouched next to her beer.

William returned with two more pints. He picked up the glass and examined the beads.

"To answer the question burning a hole through your skull, I didn't suspect right away. When your mother and I found you…it was an accident. I wasn't searching for…"

"…a werewolf?" Darkly completed the sentence.

"When I first saw the medallion around your neck, I assumed your first parents had put it on you to ward off whatever had taken them."

Darkly realized this was pretty damn close to the truth.

"And then?"

"The fact you refused to take it off, well, that seemed reasonable. If you had been told repeatedly your life depended on it, then why would you?"

"But, as it became clear the necklace caused you pain, I began to suspect another explanation. And I became convinced that it was the one thing that would enable you to lead a normal and safe life. I hoped I was doing what your first father found himself no longer in the position to do. I see you've become even more sensitive to silver."

Darkly sighed and settled back into her chair.

"Why did you let me go out there?"

"I raised you, Darkly, to be tough, to wake up and face fears and bad odds just as you would any day of the year as a Mountie. I knew it was time to let go. A little. The morning you showed up at Ennis's house, he was preparing to leave for Wolf Woods to check up on you. It was me who asked him to follow you back. It was me who sent Gus with you."

Darkly jolted forward.

"Shit. Gus."

"What's happened?" William asked, guilt in his voice. "Is he...?"

"He's not dead, Dad," Darkly said reassuringly. "But, he's not what he used to be. He's not coming home."

It was William's turn to sigh. Darkly anticipated the reason behind his concern.

"I am sure he won't let his parents think the worst. He'll find a way to get word to them. Though, maybe thinking he's dead would be easier."

"That's only one worry, Darkly. An RCMP constable goes missing, all the stops are pulled out to find him."

"Then we better get my story straight. But, Dad, that's not all. Every man, woman and child who lived in Wolf Woods has left. They've given up on isolation as their best chance of survival. They've decided if they can't beat us, they'll convert us."

Darkly realized the irony of speaking in terms of *us* and *them*. Were Buck, Marielle, and Wyatt already wearing off?

William said nothing for a good minute. He looked at the beads in the glass and then around the pub at the patrons enjoying the company of friends, unsuspecting of the multitude of hidden threats they faced every day of their existences.

"So, you're telling me we're going to see an upturn in dog bites?"

"Think lower, Dad."

Darkly settled herself back into life as an RCMP Constable. The warm weather came to an end, the leaves turned gold and red, and then the snow fell. Darkly was questioned over Gus's disappearance, then interrogated, then suspected of having some involvement in his absence. She gave him the slip, she said, in Vancouver. She didn't know what could have happened. The investigation that led her west ended up being a dead end. So, she did what she was asked to do. She took some personal time at her Uncle Ennis's place in the woods. Internal Affairs wasn't buying it.

Then something unexpected happened. Gus's parents came forward to say they had heard from their son. He was safe. He would see them again. But, he was never returning to the Mounties. They handed over a signed resignation letter. It was Gus's signature on the piece of paper. The letter had been mailed from Mexico City. Gus's parents were told that personnel at the embassy in Mexico City would make inquiries.

Darkly found the paper-pushing and public relations work she was assigned tedious. The court duty, the posing for tourists, it was all delivered out of a sense of caution. Would she have the confidence to return to action? Would she hesitate under pressure? Would a new partner trust her to have their back? So Darkly waited. Winter came to an end, and green returned to the world. Summer arrived, and the one-year anniversary of the extraordinary events at Wolf Woods came and went.

During the past year, Darkly and her father scoured the internet for incidents, clues that Buck's people had made progress in their colonization. There was always that chance that a people who led an almost institutionalized life would simply be extinguished by the modern world, unable to adapt enough to survive. But, this was wishful thinking.

The evening of October 31st rolled around, and Darkly returned home from work and microwaved her dinner. She then booted up her laptop and worked her way through the usual political and entertainment distractions to look for evidence that Wolf Woods was something beyond the figment of a personal psychosis. She came across a report of a strong earthquake in Los Angeles. The epicenter was in the Hollywood hills. Though no one was hurt, and damage was minimal, the quake was strong enough to make buildings shake, including The House of Blues music venue on Sunset Boulevard. Out of simple human interest, Darkly clicked on the video that captured the quake at the moment it happened.

A concert-goer was recording with her smartphone the band onstage in the main room at the venue. The crowd sways to the music of the pop country band, The Other Words, and a woman suddenly rushes past the camera. Then the band stops playing, and the concert-goers gasp and turn in unison to rush to the exits. The band leader onstage calls for calm, and the now shaky video ends.

Something about the course of events triggered Darkly's investigatory instincts. She played it again, then again. It was the one concert-goer running before all the rest. It reminded Darkly of the adage that animals know when natural catastrophes will hit seconds before they actual do strike.

Darkly played the video once again, hitting the pause button just as the woman running away from the stage passes the smartphone camera. The face is a little blurry, and partially covered with hair. But Darkly is pretty damn sure she is looking at the face of Marielle.

The sound of the doorbell snapped her out of her astonishment. She looked down at her untouched meal and got up, already thinking she had to get to L.A. asap. She opened her front door to a flashback.

Darkly pulled her gun on a sasquatch. The sasquatch peed its jeans. Sasquatch don't wear jeans. Darkly lowered the gun that was pointed at a teenager in a gorilla mask, holding a white pillow case full of candy open in front of her. He dropped the bag and ran.

Darkly grabbed the bag and dove back inside, slamming and locking the door.

"Fuck."

Darkly holstered her gun and dug her fingers into her hair and pulled on it. It was fucking Halloween night.

"Arghh. Stupid."

The doorbell rang again, and Darkly looked down at the bag of candy by her feet. She took a deep breath and opened the door, with the candy held out in front of her.

"I'm so sorry."

But it was not the kid returning for his Halloween loot. Ennis and Wyatt were standing there in the puddle of adolescence.

"Trick or treat," Ennis said with a grin.

Wyatt devoured the bag of Halloween candy. Wrappers hit the floor, as Ennis stood over Darkly's shoulder watching the Los Angeles earthquake video. Darkly paused over Marielle's face. Wyatt got up and inspected the face himself.

"It's her," he said, and returned to the candy.

"May I?" Ennis asked.

Darkly gave up her seat in front of the laptop and walked over to the kitchen?

"Coffee?" she called back.

"I could use something to eat," Ennis answered. "Preferably not Halloween candy."

Darkly rummaged through her fridge.

"I have some leftover Indian."

"Perfect."

Darkly emptied a couple of curry dishes and rice onto two plates and popped them into the microwave. A few minutes later, she put the plates down in front of Ennis and Wyatt and inspected what Ennis was searching for on the internet.

"Like your father and you," Ennis began, "I've been keeping an eye on the news for specific triggers. Animal attacks mainly. Upticks in STDs."

Darkly looked incredulous at this.

"You honestly think people will go to the doctor for this?"

Ennis shrugged his shoulders.

"Something did catch my eye in guess where?"

"Hollywood," Darkly guessed.

"Bingo. One of the problems of drought, which California has been in a state of now for several years, is that wild animals will move into the suburbs from the surrounding mountains in search of water and food."

"Bear, deer?"

"That's right, Darkly. Other animals, too, like mountain lions."

"I'm not following you. What do mountain lions have to do with wolves?"

Ennis pushed a couple of buttons and sat back to eat a couple bites of curry. Darkly leaned in to look at a bunch of red dots across L.A. County, California. Each dot represented a physical siting of a mountain lion in a populated area. Most of the dots were on the outskirts of L.A. proper. A few were in Santa Monica and the area around the city's iconic Griffith Park, a wilderness within one of the most urbanized areas of America.

"Are these dots, what, over five, ten years?" Darkly queried.

"Two," Ennis corrected with a full mouth. "Scroll down."

Darkly scrolled down to a new map. This one had much fewer dots.

"This one tells you the encounters with mountain lions over just the past year," Ennis continued. "See anything unusual?"

Darkly saw the same sporadic dots sprinkled around the outskirts of Los Angeles, though fewer in number. But, in the center of the city, there was a concentration of half a dozen red dots, all within a few blocks of Sunset Boulevard.

"When is the last time a mountain lion was spotted on Sunset Boulevard?" Darkly asked, suspecting the answer.

"Decades," Ennis answered, confirming her suspicion.

Darkly clicked on one of the red dots. An information bubble popped up with details of the sighting. Darkly read out loud.

"Body parts of domestic cat discovered. July. Veterinary examination revealed wounds consistent with attack by mountain lion."

"That would be kill bites to the neck or head, as opposed to bites to the hindquarters, like a coyote," Ennis interjected.

Darkly clicked on the other red dots. A homeless man's pit bull, another cat, a pet rabbit, even an iguana. Then there was the report from a night jogger, whose greyhound was snatched by something impossibly large lurking in the shadows of an alleyway. All blamed on the recent incursion by mountain lions. An incursion blamed on the drought.

"Wolves also deliver death to the neck," Darkly said with a smile that revealed she was enjoying this game. It was only just starting. "I don't believe Marielle will turn her appetites to the two-legged kind of animal. But, God only knows how many other wolves she's made. And she was pregnant. She would have had the baby by now. I wonder how many mountain lion attacks were reported on Sunset Boulevard before *the drought*?" Darkly asked cheekily.

"None," Ennis responded, with no need to check the facts online.

Darkly got up and grabbed three beers from the fridge. She gave one to Ennis and one to Wyatt. Wyatt instinctually put the bottle top in his mouth and pulled the cap off with his teeth. Darkly twisted hers off and took a drink.

"I need to get to L.A."

"Yes," Ennis concurred.

"It's time I brought Vincetti into the fold. We need someone on the inside who can cover for me. He's not going to believe this."

Ennis pointed at Wyatt.

"Seeing is believing."

Darkly knocked on the door and stepped into Sergeant Vincetti's office before he had the chance to tell her to come in or go away. He looked up and sighed internally. Darkly countered the coming patronizing placations of how her time would come, and that her current assignments were only temporary.

"I've got a lead."

Vincetti leaned back in his chair and studied Darkly for a moment.

"Okay, I'll bite. A lead on what?"

"On Gus's whereabouts."

"Has he sent another letter? Where is he now? Some other warm place fucking spring-breakers? Aruba? You know, I don't really care."

"Los Angeles."

"Good. Maybe he'll become a star. People do quit their jobs, Darkly."

"And leave the country, traveling the world without a passport?" Darkly countered, flopping down Gus's passport in front of Vincetti. "His mother gave this to me this morning."

Vincetti handed the passport back.

"He must be a dual citizen traveling on another passport."

"He's not. I looked into it."

Vincetti was becoming annoyed.

"Oh, you looked into it? Darkly, what do you care? What do any of us care? It pisses me off that a constable with a promising career ahead of him has wasted his potential and tax payers' money, but these things happen. He's not being investigated for a crime, so let it go. That's an order."

Darkly changed her line of attack.

"I didn't give Gus the slip. I was with him the whole time."

"Damnit, Darkly," Vincetti said, getting up from his chair. "Stop fucking around."

Darkly put her hands on Vincetti's desk and leaned in.

"Honest to God. We went out to a little town in the middle of nowhere, found a…," Darkly searched for words, "…cult, and he joined them."

"And why are you suddenly telling me this now?"

"I can't tell you that. But, I can show you. Join my father and me for a beer tonight."

Vincetti was at his wit's end. He walked to the door to show Darkly out.

"I don't know who put you up to this, but you can tell them to go fuck themselves. Now, get out, Darkly."

Darkly had suspected this approach wasn't going to work. But she had to try before going the difficult route. So be it. The hard way it was to be.

Vincetti pulled up the wooded driveway beyond the suburbs of Toronto. The beams from his headlights bounced off the brilliant white of the birch trees bordering the gravel drive. His home was an oasis well worth the hour and a half drive from the office and back. He was looking forward to a hot shower, a glass of wine, a little of his mother's Sunday pasta and catching a hockey game on the television. So, it was with some little fury that he got out of his car to face Darkly blocking his way to his front door. She wasn't alone. Ennis, Wyatt, and Darkly's father were with her.

"Is this supposed to intimidate me, Darkly? I'm writing you up for this."

William jumped in.

"Now, hold your horses there, son. We just want to show you something vital to national security."

"I'm not your son."

Ennis stepped forward, placing his hand on William's shoulder.

"Both William and I are retired Mounties. There was a time when that counted for something. Darkly thought if you wouldn't listen to her, you might humor a couple of old-timers."

Darkly smiled at Vincetti hopefully. He looked ready to give in, until he noticed Wyatt.

"Who's he?"

"He's what I want to show you," Darkly answered. "Can we come in?"

Vincetti brushed past the group, unlocked the door, flipped on the foyer light and left the door open for the other four to follow him in.

Vincetti pulled his jacket off and threw it on the sofa that divided the kitchen from the television room, exposing the gun holstered under his arm. The sergeant then grabbed a wine opener and removed the cork from a bottle of Italian wine and poured out five glasses. He grabbed the remote and put on the hockey he had been looking forward to watching uninterrupted.

"Well?" Vincetti asked, his eyes on the flat screen television.

Darkly took a sip of wine and set them off to the races.

"The reason Gus isn't coming back is because he was made a werewolf."

Vincetti didn't look at Darkly when he turned the television off and crossed the room for the stairs up to his bedroom.

"Finish your wine and get the hell out. I'm going to bed."

As Vincetti raised his foot onto the first step, he heard the glass shatter behind him. He swung around.

"Really?"

That was the only word he got out. Wyatt was in front of him in the space between himself and Darkly. Wyatt's fingers grew into claws, as they reached out for Vincetti. The sergeant fell onto the stairs, as hair exploded from Wyatt's face that was bubbling into a new shape. Vincetti turned and crawled up the stairwell as fast as he could. He reached the first room, the bathroom, and threw himself in, falling and hitting his head on the toilet.

Vincetti leapt back up and slammed the door shut and locked it. He stood there in the dark for a second before turning on the light to notice blood pouring from his forehead in the mirror.

"Fuck, fuck, fuck."

Vincetti grabbed some toilet paper off the roll and pressed it against his wound. It was then that the initial shock wore off and he remembered he was wearing a gun. He pulled it free of its holster and looked around him. The window was easily big enough that he could crawl out of it. He stepped into the bathtub and pushed up the window.

Thanks to the embankment on that side of the house, the drop down from the second story was only half a story. The growl that Vincetti heard outside the door was all the inspiration he needed to wiggle out the window in about two seconds and jump to the ground, where he next heard wood splintering. He felt his pockets. Damn, his car keys were in his jacket. Vincetti didn't look back. He just ran for the cover of woods.

Vincetti ran for what must have been a quarter of a mile at the fastest speed he could maintain, before he collapsed out of breath. He scrambled behind a tree and covered his body with fallen leaves. Then he listened. There was the whir of a far-off semi moving down the highway, then the click-clack of a commuter train. Vincetti forced himself to quiet his breathing to silent.

After ten minutes, he knew it was time to move again, to find his way to the road. He stood up, and it was then that a snap of a twig about a hundred feet behind him shattered the silence like a canon. Vincetti flattened himself against the tree, held his gun at the ready and waited for the next closer snap.

He was breathing heavily. He forced himself to calm, but that had the opposite effect intended. The noise of it only seemed to increase in volume. He had to get control of himself. He would kill the creature. He would kill them all if he had to.

But the breathing wasn't coming from him. He looked ahead and saw movement in the darkness. A darker shade of night that shifted position swiftly. He may not be able to see it clearly, but he knew it could see and smell *him*. It had his scent. The beast stepped into the rays of moonlight that made it through the autumn canopies. Vincetti got a full look at the large wolf. It's silver green eyes, it's yellow fangs. It was moving low to the ground, deliberately with its eyes focused on Vincetti's. Wyatt had run ahead of the sergeant and circled back to cut him off.

Vincetti raised his shaking hand to shoot. The wolf was now only fifteen feet from the kill. Just before Vincetti was to fire, Wyatt the wolf crumpled to the ground and began crawling in a circle, like he was trying to bury himself. The wolf howled and covered its face with its paws.

"Lower your weapon, sergeant."

Darkly's voice came from behind Vincetti. Behind the tree.

"It can't harm you now. It's under our control. Please, sergeant."

Vincetti slowly lowered his weapon, as William and Ennis jogged past him pointing their flashlights at Wyatt the wolf, who was in agony, but growing stiller. Vincetti noticed that Ennis had a small gold metal tube in his mouth, that the older man was blowing into. Darkly moved to Vincetti's side.

"Watch."

Wyatt the wolf passed out from pain and remained still.

"What?" was all Vincetti could muster.

"Shhh," Darkly silenced him. "Just watch."

Vincetti watched. Ennis removed the metal tube from his mouth but kept it close, ready to blow into it again. It wouldn't be necessary. The wolf appeared to melt into the ground. The hair contracted, or was it fell off the body? The man, Wyatt, whom Vincetti had met less than half an hour before was emerging from a coat of fur until all that remained was his naked body in the forest.

Ennis walked over to Vincetti and gave him a once-over.

"Clearly no harm done."

Ennis held the gold metal tube in front of Vincetti.

"My own invention. A wolf whistle. Thanks to the man you see lying on the forest floor over there, I have tested it to perfection. They can be controlled."

"Shall we go back inside?" suggested William. "I'm sure the good sergeant is finally ready to ask questions."

CHAPTER ELEVEN

"So, you're telling me they want us all to become like them?" Vincetti asked, still wrapping his head around all this.

Wyatt sat on Vincetti's sofa, wearing a blanket and devouring a pizza.

"Werewolves, yes," said Darkly, as though the word was now a common noun in the modern lexicon. "I don't suppose you could loan him some clothes?"

"What? Oh, yeah, sure."

"Sergeant," William broke in, "Darkly needs someone to cover for her and to open doors before she arrives. You put her back undercover, and only you know the true nature of the mission."

"And what do you do when you find one?" Vincetti asked the obvious.

Darkly hadn't contemplated the answer to Vincetti's question before. What did she do? She wasn't licensed to kill. She didn't want to kill anyone. Survival wasn't a crime. Why was she going after them? What was wrong with letting them get on with it? Eventually, there would be a tipping point, and all would find its way into the open organically. Oh, that's right, she thought. Then panic, social and economic collapse, war between wolves and humans, with no studio left standing to make a movie about it. It would make the Salem witch trials look like a child's slumber party.

"Every Mountie gets her man," Darkly said confidently. "I'll bring them home."

"How are you going to do that?"

"I'll become their alpha."

Darkly met Vincetti on the ferry to Centre Island. She leaned her head over the railing and let the wind rushing across the water strike her face. It was cold. It felt good. She was heading to the land of eternal sunshine. Who knew when she would experience seasons again. Vincetti slid up next to her.

Darkly turned to her sergeant and pulled him to her. She kissed him, sliding her tongue into his reluctant then willing mouth. A mother hurried her children past the lovers, hoping they wouldn't call the kissers out and bring even more attention to an uncomfortable public display of affection.

Darkly broke free of Vincetti's lips.

"You were being obvious," Darkly reprimanded her superior. "We're a couple going for a stroll on the islands. I won't like what you're going to tell me this afternoon, and we'll return on separate ferries. I'll be in tears."

"You're not in L.A. yet, Darkly."

"Undercover is undercover. Always on. If not, mistakes happen. Covers are blown."

Darkly knew the lecture would disguise her true intent. She was working Vincetti. She was about to rely on him for travel papers, contacts, and possibly rescue from extreme situations. She was betting Vincetti found her more than a little fascinating upon learning of her furry heritage. A little attention thrown his way now would make him go that extra mile to ensure there was a

future to see where all this goes. Even if Vincetti knew he was being played, Darkly felt confident enough in her own charms to
believe he would welcome it.

Darkly and Vincetti disembarked. The happy couple rented a
pedal carriage and traversed the island under the colors of autumn. During which, Vincetti filled Darkly in on her upcoming
travel. He handed over a manila envelope, which Darkly folded
and slid into her large handbag.

"I've arranged a US passport for you and proper identification
for your friend. He's a legal person now."

"Wyatt's not my friend. He's a killer with a lobotomy," Darkly
objected.

"Whatever you say. There's a contact on the LAPD. Her name's
Kathy Gutierrez. Do not contact her unless you absolutely need to.
America is a bureaucracy first and foremost. Even answering the
phone will require filling out a dozen forms on her part, and I'm
running low on favors with her. Don't piss her off."

"Got it."

They sat in silence for the next couple of minutes until Vincetti
ended it.

"Darkly, wars are lost after the fact from a badly planned peace.
What happens when you bring these…people home?"

"My father and Ennis are working on that now. There's a remote tribe in Alberta. They have the same problem as…"

"Your people?" Vincetti asked cheekily.

Darkly smiled.

"Yes. A shrinking gene pool. Perhaps they can help each other
out. Ennis's people have experience with shapeshifters."

Vincetti stopped pedaling.

"Enough. I don't want to know what else is out there. I've got
enough problems bringing drug dealers and sex traffickers to justice. You deal with that shit."

"Deal. Now, we should probably have our fight."

But, the fight did not come. The pedal carriage led to a paddle boat and then ice cream together on the ferry home. Dinner at the Beaconsfield Pub by Darkly's house came afterwards. Dinner was followed by pints and a buzzed walk home.

Darkly stood with Vincetti at her door, the key in its hole.

"That was quite the prolonged break-up," Vincetti joked.

"I'm afraid this isn't working for me. I can't see you again."

Darkly smiled and disappeared inside. Vincetti turned to leave, but before he could take a step, Darkly had opened the door and reached out for his arm. She pulled him inside and pushed him up against the closed door. She leapt into his arms, wrapped her legs around his waist and grabbed his tongue between her lips.

"Now time for the break-up sex."

Vincetti carried Darkly to her sofa and threw her down. He quickly peeled her jeans off her and buried his face between her legs. Darkly had not been with a man since her first visit to Wolf Woods, and it didn't take long for her succumb to her sergeant's talents.

Darkly pulled Vincetti up on top of her and kissed him deeply while she undid his belt. Just grabbing hold of him made her feel a wave of pleasure.

But, as she was about to guide him into her - she hoped repeatedly through the night - another thought crept into her mind. The cure. Since removing the medallion that saved her from the curse, her senses had become more acute. Other changes, too, had occurred. Animalistic tendencies. She had even found herself resisting the urge to hunt. She had followed a young office worker from downtown to the suburbs one night, overcome by the desire to taste him. As in bite him. She withdrew at the last minute, stopping herself from pounding on his front door and settling for rare calf's liver and onions.

"Stop!" she shouted.

With the changes occurring within her, did that mean she could now spread the curse? She pushed Vincetti off her, and he toppled over onto the floor.

"Seriously, Darkly?"

"You need to leave."

"What the hell?"

Darkly pulled her jeans back on and pulled Vincetti up off the floor. He stood there, naked from the waist down. She wanted what she saw, but she had the public good to think about. It took precedence even over primal instincts.

"Be grateful you aren't any bigger. Another half inch, and you might have found me chaining you up in the basement each full moon. We can't take a chance."

With Vincetti fully dressed, sexually frustrated, and in an uber headed home, Darkly spent what she assumed would be the last night in her apartment for a long time. What did her in-between state mean for her love life? If she slept with a mere human, she risked spreading the disease. If she slept with a wolf, she risked catching a disease she sometimes thought she desired and other times didn't. There are condoms. But condoms are never one hundred percent effective. This was getting complicated.

Darkly's father saw her off at the airport. He handed her the wolf whistle Ennis had designed. She wasn't going to rely on that alone.

William sat next to Darkly, while she waited for her flight to board. Being a distinguished, retired RCMP constable had its privileges, like passing through security without a boarding pass and both father and daughter moving through the airport's US Customs with little more than a nod. Dealing with such formalities on the Canadian side of the border made Darkly's and every other traveler's journey a hell of a lot easier.

"Your mother is planning a Victorian Christmas this year."

"What does that mean?"

"Extra work for me."

Darkly knew her father was planning their next meeting like a self-fulfilling prophecy. She gave him what he was fishing for.

"I'll be there."

"Good."

The pre-boarding announcement for Darkly's flight to L.A. broke the moment of family bonding.

"Darkly."

"Dad."

William took the hand of the only daughter he had ever known.

"From my time in the arctic, I learned that those we fear are sometimes the ones who need protecting the most."

William watched his daughter board the plane and then left, certain Darkly's task would not be completed before Christmas.

Darkly had been to Los Angeles in the past for an international law enforcement conference. She had not found it to be the odd mix of ambition and delusion she had read about. To her, it was Americana at its purest. Suburban neighborhoods, swimming pools, dream factories and eternal sunshine. It was the movies come to life.

Vincetti's reach extended to L.A., and he had arranged for her first guardian angel to meet her. Darkly stepped into the line at the Starbucks in Terminal 7 of LAX. She spotted the nametag of the young African-American preparing what looked like a cappuccino. She walked past the cash register and leaned on the counter to speak with *Xander*.

"Do you know what a double-double is?" she asked him.

Darkly's code words for announcing her arrival were commonplace where she was from. But in America, two sugars and two creams were just that and nothing shorter.

Xander looked up and said without hesitation, "Lady, are you hitting on me?"

Darkly covered her jaw with her hand, as the sensation of a toothbrush made with bristles of steel wool spread across the roof of her mouth. She forced a smile for the killer standing in front of her and regained her composure.

"Never mind," Darkly replied and walked away.

Darkly ended up at one of the baggage carousels and waited for a bag that wasn't coming. After five minutes of standing, she spotted several seats at the last exit on the arrivals level and parked herself.

As the last person on her flight left with their luggage, Xander appeared, holding a small brown paper bag with the iconic Starbucks mermaid on it. He dropped the bag in the garbage can next to the row of seats Darkly was planted on, then walked out the exit without looking at her.

Darkly took another look around, got up and with the speed of a toddler on sugar, yanked the bag out of the garbage and opened it to remove a croissant. She bit into the bread and glanced up at the security camera that hovered over that part of the airport, then followed the licensed killer out the exit. This was an easy assignment for him, Darkly thought, as Xander stopped to light a cigarette. Darkly walked past him, holding the croissant for him to clearly see, but not making eye contact. She parted the heavy airport traffic at a crosswalk and headed for the parking structure directly across from arrivals.

Once Darkly was in the elevator, she tore the croissant apart to remove an automobile key fob. The elevator beeped at the second level, and Darkly got off. She walked down the aisles of cars, pressing the red alarm button on the key fob. Nothing. On the third level, Darkly struck gold and climbed into a blue Toyota Prius.

With the doors locked, Darkly opened the glove compartment and removed a small handgun, which she dropped into her oversized handbag full of toiletries and clean panties. Also in the glove compartment, was an iPhone and a wad of fifty dollar bills.

Darkly plugged the phone into the console and opened the navigation app. She tapped the only entry in the history and started the engine.

Paul Nabor loved being a scoutmaster. It was something normal and wholesome in a town that dreaded the usual. He had risen all the way to Eagle Scout himself back in Indiana, and he was determined to stay involved in the organization whether his girlfriend and he ended up having kids or not. Paul discovered that many of his friends remembered their Boy Scout days fondly, and were eager to turn their sons over to Paul's care once a week. A *Good Nabor*, they called him.

Paul's yearly night hike through Griffith Park had become legendary. On its fifth anniversary, a local news crew accompanied the kids, and then everyone wanted to put their son in Paul's troop. He now had a waiting list.

On this autumn night, Paul led the troop up one of the wide trails that would eventually bring them to the base of Griffith Observatory. The canyon trail was noisy with coyote and insect calls. Upon setting off, Paul had encouraged the boys to only think of the flashlight as a tool to stop them from tripping on a root. The real experience would come through their ears. Without the distraction of too much sight, the world of the night would open itself up to the boys, and they would understand that the second largest city in the country was full of wild things.

They had no idea how wild things could get.

Darkly followed the GPS to a flat above Echo Lake Reservoir. It took her a further twenty minutes driving around the neighborhood to find a parking spot. But, three hours after sundown, Darkly found herself at a front door with an electronic keypad above the keyhole. She opened the notes app on her phone and found the only note, which was six numbers, each divided by a space.

Darkly punched the numbers into the keypad, and the whir of a tumbler turning told her the apartment was hers. She turned the doorknob and walked into a comfortable one-bedroom with all the amenities of home. Darkly even found a full fridge. She inspected a cold bottle of bubble tea. There was little she found quite so upsetting as opaque drinks. Darkly's tastes were definite and unaccommodating.

Darkly gave herself a tour of the living and sleeping areas. Xander, or another agent from a service Darkly knew better than to question, had put fresh sheets on the bed and stocked the bathroom with anything an undercover cop might need on assignment, including boxes of hair color of every possible shade.

Darkly returned to the kitchen and opened the freezer. She removed the ice collector from the ice maker and dumped the ice out into the sink. A plastic sandwich bag was the last thing to fall out. In it, Darkly found several IDs in her own name. There was a California driver's license, a Social Security Card, and a US birth certificate.

Darkly admired the photos of herself. They were recent. There was nothing these people couldn't get. She removed the IDs she had traveled to L.A. on from her handbag and put them in the sandwich bag, which she placed in the bottom of the ice receptacle and returned to the freezer.

Darkly made herself an omelet and went to bed, eager to sleep for eight hours under the knowledge that only one or two other people knew her exact location. She could relax and lose herself, even if only for a night.

Scoutmaster Paul Nabor was approaching the summit of the hike. One of the two telescope housings loomed in the dark above them. The dark outline was just visible against the dim light of the stars. The observatory was closed for short-term renovations, so Paul and his kids should have the lawn in front of the facility to themselves. It was a great night for a lesson about the constellations.

But, Paul was mistaken. They were not alone. It was one of his youngest scouts who saw it first. In his first year of scouting, the boy remained close to Paul the entire hike. His flashlight caught the glow of eyes up ahead in the trail, and then a tail and fur, as something long slinked off into the brush.

"I just saw a coyote, I think," said the boy.

"Stop," whispered Paul to the other boys.

The troop quieted and huddled around Paul, who was scanning the brush on the side of the trail for what the boy had seen. To his surprise, his flashlight beam bounced off two large eyes.

"Shhh," the scoutmaster commanded.

There was nothing to silence. He had every boy's attention. He couldn't believe it. There was a coyote watching them. A brave fellow. A big fellow, too, thought Paul, as the boys aimed their lights on the spot their scoutmaster was focused. They lit up the face of the animal. Its fur was a bluish silver. Paul immediately noticed the wide face, rounded ears, and jaw that was not as pointed as it should be. This had to be a stray German Shepherd or a coyote and dog mix.

The canine whined and lowered its head.

"I think we have found a stray dog, lads," Paul.

There was a collective sigh of disappointment from the scouts.

"He's probably scared, aren't you, boy?"

Paul lifted a small backpack off his back and removed a granola bar.

"He can smell the coyotes. He probably wandered into the park when it was light. But, if we don't help him find his way out, he runs the risk of being eaten."

"Eaten?" asked one of the scouts with alarm.

"Domestic animals are an easy source of food for coyotes. They're predators. They're only doing what nature made them for. Every animal on this planet, including us, is programmed to seek out the easiest food source. Though from the look of the size of this guy, it would take the whole pack to bring him down."

Paul unwrapped the granola bar and held it out for what he thought was a lost pet.

"Come on, boy. We're not going to hurt you. Come on. Show us your tag."

Paul stepped closer to the dog, waved the bar in the air and then set it down on the ground.

The dog stepped back deeper into the brush and disappeared.

"Well, that's that. I'm not going in after it. Let's keep moving."

Paul motioned to the walls of the observatory above them.

"Almost there."

Just as they resumed the hike, there was an ungodly commotion in the brush. Snarls followed by growls followed by jaws snapping followed by yelps. A pack had found the stray, and war ensued.

Paul ushered the boys back to the opposite edge of the trail from the commotion.

"Stand back. We're not in any danger. They don't attack humans."

At that moment, the boys were given reason to think otherwise when six coyotes came bolting out of the bush, snapped and barked at the scouts, and then ran down the hill, two of them limping.

The scouts and their leader were frozen in shock. This was more nature than anyone had anticipated. After a minute, Paul broke the silence and refocused the boys on the climb.

"Okay. This has been a memorable night."

That was the cue for boys to let loose. Laughing and excited chatter continued for the rest of the hike up to the observatory. Paul led the boys around the final corner up onto the lawn in front of the iconic monument from the golden age of Hollywood, celebrating its love of the stars in the sky, as well as the stars in the hills.

The building was dark, and scaffolding obscured much of the elegance of the building's curves. The security shed on the other side of the observatory lawn was also dark, and the parking lot was filled with skips of building debris.

"Let's look at the light show, gentlemen," Paul said, leading the troop to the railing that overlooked the canyon below and the Hollywood sign on the next hill over.

Hollywood stretched out below them, and, in the distance, the streetlights of Santa Monica ended at the blanket of blackness that is the Pacific Ocean. Paul felt the urge to whip around. The primitive instinct that told human ancestors they were being stalked grabbed hold of the scoutmaster.

Paul scanned the lawn and astronomers monument with his flashlight. Nothing. He checked his watch. It was time to call the mothers with minivans and carry them all back down the hill.

"Before we go, can anyone name the six astronomers the monument was built as a tribute to?"

But before Paul's question could be answered, the largest dog anyone in the troop had likely ever seen, appeared from behind the monument and sat its hindquarters down on the lawn. It stared at Paul and the boys and bared its teeth. The animal's low growl carried on the air over to the troop, and the boys instinctually moved as a group to behind Paul.

If Paul didn't know any better, he would swear he was looking at a wolf. But, that was impossible.

The dog, or wolf, then got up on all fours and walked slowly toward Paul, teeth still bared. This thing was attacking. It loped a couple paces, and Paul and the boys backed themselves into the railing. Then the wolf slowed to a creeping pace again.

Paul had no time to think. If he had, he may have told the boys to run for the skips and climb on top of the debris to fight the wolf off with boards and pipes. Or, he may have thought to run for the security hut, kick in the door and hide there until sunup.

But, all that came to mind was to charge the animal and distract it from attacking the boys.

"Okay. Now listen up. You all remember how we got up here. It's a lot easier and faster going down."

Paul made eye contact with the oldest boy, who was covered in merit badges.

"Jarrod, you're in charge. I'm going to distract the dog and draw it away. You make sure everyone makes it down in one group. You move quietly back to the trail. Understood?"

"Yes sir," Jarrod answered.

Paul put his hand on Jarrod's shoulder.

"Make sure everyone stays together."

Jarrod nodded.

"Turn your flashlights off, and start moving now. Don't turn them back on until you're halfway down the trail."

Every flashlight clicked off, except for Paul's. Paul charged the animal and flung his canteen, hitting the canine square between the eyes. It whelped and backed up.

"Go," Paul yelled to Jarrod.

As the boys made their way back to the trailhead, the wolf regained its composure and focused on Paul's light, as Paul hoped it would. The wolf stalked the scoutmaster once again, and Paul backed up quickly, leading the wolf to the observatory steps, as his troop disappeared silently down the trail.

Paul and the wolf kept the same pace, and the scoutmaster reached the winding stone stairwell that led to one of the two telescope housings. He climbed over the low cast iron gate and backed up the steps. As he reached the bend in the stairwell, the wolf leapt over the gate and followed Paul slowly up the steps.

Paul lost sight of the wolf as he turned the bend of the circular stairwell. He then hurried the rest of the way up to the roof and look-out. Paul had an unobstructed view of the entire L.A. basin below. Millions of people out there, and none of them could help him. He turned back to the stairwell and waited for the wolf that would appear any moment. But, it didn't appear. Thirty seconds passed, and then thirty more.

He looked back out over the city. In the canyon below, much to his relief, he saw one light, then several, then all the flashlights of his troop turn on. They were moving quickly as a group to safety, as he had instructed. He thought this was the time to join them. The drop down to the tree tops couldn't be more than a story. Then he could climb down a tree to the ground and race in darkness down a path he had trodden more times than he could count.

Paul directed his light into the canyon to find a landing spot and caught sight of something he never expected. Looking up at him were four faces. These faces were connected to naked bodies. There were two young men, a young woman and a middle-aged woman.

"What the f…"

But he didn't complete the thought. The hairs on the back of Paul's neck leapt to attention, he spun around to see the wolf leaping for his head. Paul put his hands in front of his face in one final futile act of self-preservation. The weight of the wolf slamming into him catapulted the young scoutmaster with most of his life still in front of him off the Griffith Observatory roof and into the canyon below.

Paul heard his own neck snap when he missed the tree canopies and landed on the rocks below. He was dead less than a second later. Just as well. No one should experience being eaten alive.

About twenty minutes later, Jarrod led the troop out of the park onto Los Feliz Boulevard, where he flagged down an L.A. police cruiser and officially triggered the biggest local news story of the year.

CHAPTER TWELVE

Darkly had barely slept. Nightmares. Each was a variation on the same theme. She was running, driving, sitting on the sofa. In each scenario, in the sky, out the window, was a moon growing ever larger in the sky. It grew to the size that its brightness became blinding, enveloping Darkly's body with a feverish heat. She pulled her clothes apart, but her naked body offered no relief. At the moment of feeling like she would burst into flames, Darkly would wake, sweating profusely.

At six in the morning, Darkly ended her last dream, got up and rummaged around her bottomless pit of a handbag for a pair of speedos and a t-shirt. She went for a run around the Echo Park reservoir and grabbed a coffee and muffin from a local, organic, fair trade shop run by an over-privileged blonde woman who told Darkly the coffee she was about to enjoy had been blessed by a shaman. Darkly knew a thing or two about shamans, so it wasn't the selling point the proprietor had hoped for.

Back at her flat, Darkly showered and then sat down in front of the TV in the living area to eat her muffin. Every local channel had the same news. The morning was owned by a scout troop from Los Feliz, and by their scoutmaster, whose partially-eaten body was discovered in the canyon below Griffith Observatory.

A young, Latina reporter stood in front of a road barrier, with a sign hanging from it that read *Park Closed.*

"I had the opportunity to speak with a parent of one of the scouts, who had this to say about the tragic night's events."

The picture on the television cut away to the front door of a suburban home. The same reporter held a mic in front of a man in his forties, who was unshaven, with bags under his eyes.

"My son says it was a big dog. A coyote, I guess. Maybe a hybrid dog and coyote. Who knows. Paul was a godsend. They don't make many men like him. He lived for those boys. If a family couldn't afford camping supplies for their kid, they came out of his pocket."

The dad shook his head, and the location switched back to the park and the reporter on her own.

"A selfless man who had conducted this night hike many times before. So, what went wrong this time? Today, L.A. Animal Control will conduct a sweep of the park, in search of an unusually large coyote. Any coyotes caught will be destroyed as a precaution. If rabies is to blame for such a display of animal aggression, officials say that containing the outbreak to Griffith Park must be the priority in the days ahead."

Darkly turned the television off and addressed her reflection in the shiny black screen.

"Goddammit. You were too late. You failed. You couldn't save a fish from a frying pan, Darkly Stewart. Fuck me!"

Darkly made her way almost immediately to Griffith Park. She made one stop on Western Avenue, where she stepped into a pawn shop t0 buy a pair of binoculars. She then drove to the Los Angeles Zoo parking lot and joined the throngs of families and couples making a day of it with the animals.

Darkly purchased a single admission ticket and found a quiet bench, from which to study the complimentary map. She soon found what she was looking for.

Twenty-five minutes later, Darkly confidently slipped under a road barrier and walked up a service road that ran behind cages of small primates from South America. Certain that no one was looking, the Mountie left the road for the place she was most comfortable: in the bush.

Darkly carved her own trail up the base of Mount Hollywood until, just a little out of breath, she reached a proper trail, which she joined and traveled for a steady, relaxed hour before branching off onto a bridle path and taking that the rest of the way to the summit.

No other hikers were encountered on the trek, and Darkly was certain all trails had been closed at their beginnings in deference to the investigation taking place in the park. Above her, three helicopters circled the mountain. Darkly felt safe from the peering eyes of the news and police copters. She had found a pair of camouflage pants close enough to her size, along with a tan-colored top in the closet of her home away from home. She blended in perfectly with her surroundings.

The bridle path brought Darkly to an intersection of several hiking trails just below the mountain's summit. Below her were the skylines of Burbank and Glendale, and over the summit would be Hollywood.

Darkly didn't climb any further, but made her way covertly around the summit, remaining hidden within the small desert trees and succulents until she reached a spot that gave her as clear a view of the observatory as she could hope for. Darkly raised the binoculars around her neck to view the commotion below. The observatory lawn was filled with Mercedes utility vehicles marked with the words *L.A. Animal Control* on the sides.

Wafting up from the unseen canyon below the observatory was smoke. It wasn't the smoke of a fire, but more like a controlled fog.

Animal control officers emerged from the canyon trail carrying coyote bodies, either passed out or dead from the smoke, and deposited them in the utility vehicles.

"Pointless," said Darkly aloud to herself.

There wasn't a coroner's vehicle, or much of a plainclothes force. This was a clean-up operation. The coyotes would take the blame, gassed and dragged from their dens, then extinguished, and the park would be declared safe once again. A tragic, freakish, once-in-a-generation accident of fate that would go down in Hollywood lore, to be marched out and retold every Halloween season. There was sure to be a docudrama made about the scout troop.

Nothing more could be learned from this vantage point. Darkly needed to get closer. So, she settled in for a rest, hoping the rattlesnakes were already in hibernation mode, and waited for nightfall.

Full-on darkness came not long after 5pm. Darkly ate a pack of child's fruit gummies she bought in the zoo. It suddenly popped into her head that her car would be towed after closing. She really couldn't afford to bring attention to herself, but this was more important. She would just have to hope for the best.

The clearance operation continued below, with floodlights mounted on the observatory roof lighting up the canyon, when Darkly made her way carefully down to the lawn, a light black jacket she had carried with her zipped up tightly to her neck. Part of her thought the best thing to do was walk through the clutter of cube vans and the city's middle management, as though she belonged there. It had worked for her before. Nowhere better to hide than in plain sight. But, her gut told her it wasn't going to work this time.

After jumping between official vehicles and avoiding the eyelines of bored uniformed cops in patrol cars, Darkly dove down a narrow trailhead that began at the corner of the observatory's parking lot. Lights had been set up throughout the canyon, so the terrain was illuminated enough for her not to worry about falling down a steep gully. They also illuminated the smoke used to incapacitate the coyotes, giving the whole place an otherworldly look. Darkly shone a small penlight on the trail in front of her. She was looking for prints.

As she wound her way along the trail, Darkly could hear the growls and whelps of drugged coyotes being dragged from dens in the ground. Shooting them would have been more efficient, thought Darkly. Though, she wouldn't want to be in the vicinity of a green officer firing his weapon at a wild animal in the dark for the first time.

Darkly was getting close to the sound of human voices. Twenty more yards, and she'd need to turn back. It was another five yards, when Darkly spotted them. The dirt was dry. It never rained in southern California, as the song goes. But, Darkly was adept at picking up the faintest tracks. Plus, the park had been closed to public traffic all day, meaning there was little chance of the ground being disturbed. At least where the police hadn't trodden.

She bent down to get a closer look. She was certain. They were the paw pads of a canine. And she thought she could just make out the points of claws. Darkly placed her hand next to the faint print. It was the size of her own hand. A little bigger, actually. That's no coyote.

"Stand up slowly."

The voice came from behind Darkly. A man's voice, firm and annoyed. Darkly stood up and raised her hands to where the officer could see them.

"You fucking death hounds. It's really sick, you know. Put your hands behind your back."

Darkly did as he said and didn't respond. First rule: don't provoke. The officer handcuffed Darkly and turned her around to shine his flashlight in her face.

"A man died here. He was ripped to pieces. I saw the body. Any more tourists of the macabre with you?"

Tourists of the macabre. Good one. Worth remembering. Darkly would use it in the future when she found herself in the same situation as this young Hollywood cop.

"No, sir, officer."

"I'm going to step behind you because the trail isn't wide enough for me to escort you to the top. I will shine the light in front of you, and you will feel my palm on your upper back. This is for your safety only. Do you understand?"

"Yes," Darkly answered.

"Good. Please begin walking. Slowly. This isn't a race. I'm on duty all night."

Darkly found the jail cell amusing. She had the cell to herself. There were no hookers from Sunset Boulevard or movie stars busted for drunk driving. It wasn't at all what she was hoping for from a Hollywood arrest. It was clean. The bench had built-in padding. She had even gotten a little sleep. It was 8am, when a guard came and unlocked the door and called her name.

"Darkly Stewart?"

She looked around her.

"I guess."

"Funny," the guard replied. "I haven't heard that one before. I'm to take you upstairs to see Lieutenant Gutierrez. Come on."

Darkly was escorted up nondescript stairs, without the handcuffs being reapplied. A couple of flights up, the guard reached around her and opened a door for her. She walked into a room full of desks with plainclothes officers sitting drinking coffee and working on computers. None were remotely interested in Darkly's presence.

"To the end of the hall. There's an interview room on the left."

At that point, the guard stopped and turned his attention to an ancient Mister Coffee machine. He poured himself a coffee in a Styrofoam cup.

"She's waiting for you in there," the guard said while stirring the powdered non-dairy creamer he'd just poured into the coffee.

"That stuff will kill you," Darkly offered.

The guard looked at her with zero emotion, and Darkly continued her walk to the interview room. She understood now that this was a walk of shame. Kathy had spoken with Vincetti, and she was making sure that Darkly knew she had wasted valuable police time by marching her through one of the busiest floors in the station.

Darkly knocked on the interview room door and stepped inside. Lieutenant Gutierrez wasn't what Darkly expected. She had a sensual Latina woman in mind. Again, Hollywood was corrupting Darkly's grasp on reality. What she came up against was a rather severe, all-business woman with short-cropped, yet fashionable hair, wearing a pantsuit more appropriate for politicians than police officers.

"Constable."

Gutierrez greeted Darkly with the one word. No emotion. That was a thing here. No judgment in her voice. Just acknowledgment that she knew who Darkly was, and that she had some explaining to do as to what Darkly was doing on her turf.

"Please have a seat."

Darkly sat down at a metal table across from Gutierrez. The lieutenant was working through a pile of manila folders. Darkly understood these were props to once again communicate to Darkly that she was a busy woman who had better things to do than question snooping law enforcement officers from other countries.

Gutierrez continued to jot down notes on a piece of paper for the next minute, before clicking her pen, closing the folder and looking up at Darkly.

"Welcome to L.A., Constable Darkly Stewart."

"Thank you."

Darkly returned the smile she received from Gutierrez. She rubbed her thumb and index finger together. The scans of her fingerprints would have turned up exactly who she was.

"Sergeant Vincetti tells me you're here on vacation. Into hiking at night on your vacations? In the middle of restricted police investigations?"

"It's a hobby."

Darkly thought she should go with the humor angle first. Gutierrez leaned back in her chair, making clear she was still awaiting an explanation.

"I arrived night before last," Darkly began to explain.

"On a United flight from Toronto, connecting in Denver," Gutierrez finished for her.

"Yes. And I was just as shocked as the rest of L.A. to wake up on the first morning of my…"

"Vacation," continued Gutierrez.

"…and hear the tragic news on the television about the scout troop. I didn't think much about it, at first. Despite where your officers found me, I didn't come here for the hiking. I get plenty of that in my job. But, I couldn't help but think it was really strange that a man was killed by a coyote."

"We think it was a coyote-dog hybrid," Gutierrez corrected.

"Right. But, killed? Ripped to pieces, I believe the officer who arrested me said?"

"And your point, Constable?"

"It was the suggestion that it was bigger than a coyote that jogged my memory. There was a case in Canada before my time. An extremist green group released wolves into city parks. Heavily wooded parks."

Darkly had Gutierrez's interest.

"Were there any deaths?"

"No. Not even on the wolf side. They were tranquilized and returned to the wolf sanctuaries they had been abducted from. But the activists were never tracked down."

Gutierrez leaned forward.

"Wait. You think that's what this is?"

"No. Well, I thought, maybe it could be. A copycat. But, I was wrong. I found some large prints. They were definitely from a domestic dog. German Shepherd, Mastiff, some such breed. I don't think it's a hybrid you're looking for."

Darkly was lying. The question was, could Gutierrez tell?

"You should have come to the police with this information rather than investigate your hunch. This isn't your jurisdiction. This isn't even the border."

Now Gutierrez was laying down the law.

"I'm sorry. There's no excuse for my actions, Lieutenant Gutierrez. All I can say is it's hard not to investigate, when that's your job."

Gutierrez got up, picked up the stack of manila folders and walked to the door.

"Try not to follow your instincts from now on. While you're in my hometown. In fact, do more than try, or I'll have you deported. You're free to go."

Gutierrez opened the door.

"Oh. You said you didn't come here to hike. What did you come to Los Angeles for, Constable?"

"The music scene," Darkly answered without hesitation.

Darkly got an uber back to the zoo and found her car where she had left it, but with a parking ticket on the windshield. She'd been lucky. She needed to be a lot more careful moving forward. There was still a wolf in L.A. At least one. Darkly was convinced. She was also certain Lieutenant Kathy Gutierrez would be keeping an eye on her.

CHAPTER THIRTEEN

Darkly spent the next day lying low. She hit a couple classic rock 'n' roll joints, lunching at Bob's Beanery, where she drank beer in the same spot Jim Morrison supposedly propped up the bar. She saw an 80's hair band at The Greek, and took the obligatory tour of stars' homes in the Hollywood hills. That was by day.

By night, Darkly scoured the music venues along the Sunset strip: House of Blues, Whisky-A-Go-Go, The Viper Room, The Roxy. She was looking for Marielle, or anyone she might recognize from Wolf Woods. After a week, she came up empty. During that same time, Griffith Park had seen its colony of coyotes exterminated, and the hiking trails reopened. Darkly took a chance and returned to the park and walked the trail where she had turned up the wolf tracks. There were no more to be found.

So, it was, on the eighth night of her so-called vacation, Darkly happened into a bar too cool for a sign above the door. There was just a large nose crafted out of copper wire. Achoo was its name. Minimalist gray on the inside, with a stunning mahogany bar that dominated the center of the front lounge. Behind it, was a large open area for congregating and dancing, with a stage that lined the back wall beyond that.

It was 9pm, and the place was filling up. Darkly got the bartender's attention easily. He wore the California uniform for such a place: man bun, suspenders, beard. He passed by several waiting customers to get Darkly a rum and coke.

"Who's playing?" she asked the hipster as he placed her drink down in front of her.

"Moonkill," he replied.

"They any good?"

The bartender shrugged his shoulders and moved on to the next paying customer. So, Darkly made her way to the back of the crowd of attentive, swaying bodies. The music wasn't bad. It might even be considered good, if it wasn't for the fact that it sounded a little too reminiscent of music twenty years previous. But, hey, the 90's are making a comeback, she thought.

She got a glimpse of the lead-singer through the bobbing heads. He looked vaguely familiar, so they must have made enough of a name for themselves to reach her out-of-touch ears.

Darkly politely pushed her way through the fans up to the stage. The band consisted of the lead-singer, a young woman on the keyboard, a guy on the drums and another on the bass guitar. She got a better look at the singer. His hair was wet with sweat and covered his eyes. He was kind of geeky looking, but muscular. Not conventionally attractive, but projected magnetism. It was the guitar, concluded Darkly. Put a guitar in the hands of a five, and he becomes a seven or eight.

Darkly caught a glimpse of a hip middle-aged woman out of the corner of her eye. Her eyes were glued to Darkly, who was quite happy to make eye contact back. Darkly suspected it was one of Gutierrez's people. The woman was dressed immaculately in flawless blue jeans, black leather jacket and black cowboy boots. Her skin was flawless and wrinkle-free, but her eyes spoke of age beyond her years. The woman smiled and then turned her attention back to the lead-singer. She stepped forward to lean against the stage, revealing Marielle, who had been standing hidden beside the woman out of sight.

Marielle took one look at Darkly and bolted. Concertgoers and beer went flying, as Marielle made her escape. Darkly aimed for the front door, in an attempt to cut Marielle off after she made it around the bar. But, at the bar, Marielle turned and headed for the toilets. Darkly changed course and made it to the hallway that led to the women's room, just as the door slammed shut.

Darkly was at the door two seconds later and kicked it open. She immediately took stock of her surroundings. Two sinks, three toilet stalls, and an open window. Did she squeeze out the open window first, or check the stalls? She punched each stall open, one by one. No one. That took three seconds.

She then leapt up onto one of the sinks, knocking the cold water tap cap off. Water sprayed everywhere, and Darkly hauled herself outside. She was just barely able to fit through the window, so she knew Marielle could fit too. Darkly dropped down into an alleyway a couple of feet below. She turned to her left. There were three plastic garbage bins and a brick wall. To the right, was a chain link gate that joined a fence that stretched over Darkly's head, covering the entire alleyway. It was a cage. The gate was locked with chains.

Darkly flipped the lids to the garbage bins and pulled out bags of trash. No Marielle.

"What?"

Maybe she hid in the men's room? But Darkly saw the door to the women's room shut. Someone entered. Darkly climbed back into the women's room to face a couple of girls dressed to the nines, out for a night of clubbing. They were standing clear of the spray of water from the sink that was now drenching Darkly.

"Somebody should really fix that. There's a drought," she said with disgust and walked out of the toilet right into the lead-singer of Moonkill.

"Whoa. Sorry," he apologized.

"No problem."

He noticed Darkly's wet hair.

"Did you take a bath in there?"

"I'm sorry?"

Darkly felt her hair and realized she was really wet.

"Ah. Sink's broken."

Darkly nodded and moved past the singer who was smiling and shaking his head. She searched every inch of the club, until banging on the men's toilet stalls to order everyone out got her escorted to the front door by the bouncer.

She'd found Marielle. And lost her again.

The next morning, Darkly went for her run around the reservoir and put her thinking cap on. She had to assume that Marielle was the wolf in Griffith Park. And she had to assume she was tracking a murderer. But what would she do with her when she caught up with her? Turn Marielle into Kathy Gutierrez and say *you're welcome?* Darkly promised her father and Vincetti that she would return the were-folk home. Of course, Wolf Woods was overrun by sasquatch. Ennis said he could house a few werewolves, while he searched for another ghost town to renovate. But, how would she entice or force so many to return? And how would she keep them there once she got them back? She had few answers.

Darkly soon concluded that she would need to tranquilize Marielle for the journey back. She'd drive to the Canadian border and then rely on Vincetti to get her and a woman who, as far as any government official is concerned, doesn't exist into British Columbia. As for the rest of the wolves, she needed to find Buck. If she could convince him, she could convince the rest. She had an idea about that. She was willing to go as far as a woman can go to convince Buck to give up his current course.

Darkly decided she would concentrate on the task at hand for now. She needed to bring Marielle to justice. The girl was on alert now and would surely behave herself knowing that Darkly was around. It wasn't going to be easy, but the werewolf would eventually slip up.

Darkly grabbed her ritual coffee and stepped out of the shop, only to run into the lead-singer of Moonkill for the second time.

"Excuse me," the singer said.

Darkly thrust the coffee out to the side to avoid splashing her or the singer with scalding coffee. She took an intake of breath and waited for the worst. But, all was okay.

"I'm so sorry. Did you burn yourself?" the singer urgently enquired.

"No, I'm alright," Darkly answered.

She didn't hide her annoyance very well.

"Oh. I've made you spill half your coffee. Here, let me get you a fresh one."

"That's okay. I should cut back on the caffeine anyway."

"No, really, I insist. I'm buying you a coffee whether you drink it or not. Wait a minute. You're the lady who's all wet."

"And you're with the band. Moonkill."

It came to Darkly's mind that this guy could be useful.

"With? I am Moonkill. I write the music and lyrics. Name's Toma."

Toma held out one hand for Darkly and held the door to the coffee shop open with the other. Darkly accepted his hand and the door.

"Darkly."

"Darkly. I like that. What'll you have, Darkly? Cappuccino? Latte?"

"Just standard American coffee. Black."

"Got it."

Toma bought Darkly a new cup of coffee and himself a dirty chai latte.

They took a seat at a table outside the front door, where Toma went right for the jugular.

"What did you think of the band?"

Darkly knew exactly how to play this.

"Good."

"Good?" Toma asked with a strong undercurrent of disappointment.

"Truth is I barely heard anything. I was just there looking for someone."

"Well, I'll tell you what, Moonkill is playing The Cha Cha Lounge tomorrow night. Why don't you come? I'll put you on the list. You can listen this time. If you don't find someone first."

Darkly walked home alone. She'd agreed to show up at Toma's next show. But there was a thought creeping into Darkly's mind. It was no accident that Toma bumped into her at the coffee shop. He'd followed her home last night. She had a stalker, and he knew where she lived. He seemed harmless enough. There were no warning signs going off in her mouth. Not even an antiseptic mouthwash burn. She'd cut him loose eventually. In the meantime, there was nothing wrong with a little platonic fling.

After a shower, Darkly reviewed the earthquake footage and studied Marielle's face once again. Something wasn't right. She looked scared, and Darkly wasn't convinced it was because of the earthquake. The Mountie in her knew when someone feared for their life. The quality of the video wasn't great, but Darkly also thought she noticed bruising around one of Marielle's eyes. Was she sporting a shiner?

Darkly returned to Sunset Boulevard that night. But not to hear the latest in indie rock. She knew what happened to young women in a new town, with no prospects. Darkly went soliciting prostitutes, armed with a wad of $50 bills and a print-out of Marielle's face.

She drove around Hollywood, looking for the tell-tale signs of the oldest profession. The tight uniform, the eye make-up, the teased hair, the darkened doorways of closed-up shops. She spoke with any girl who would speak with her. It broke Darkly's heart to see how young some of the girls were, and how little a grasp Los Angeles had on the scourge of sex trafficking. But all questions turned up nothing on Marielle. Darkly believed each woman, when they told her they'd never seen Marielle before.

Darkly spent the rest of the night slipping in and out of bars and diners. She was certain that Marielle was sustaining herself under cover of night. Perhaps Marielle's situation was one in which money was not an issue. If so, that raised an interesting possibility, like a patron or protector. A patron able to frighten a werewolf?

Darkly decided she would take the day off. She had a date to see a rock star that night. Well, a musician with promise. She'd get her nails and hair done and take an afternoon siesta, so she could make a night of it.

With all the pre-show preparations accomplished, Darkly arrived early at the Cha Cha Lounge in the trendy L.A. neighborhood of Silver Lake. So, she crossed the road to The Red Lion pub. Darkly's adopted name, Schilling, meant she'd developed a taste for schnitzel, German beer, and everything pickled. German tapas, as Darkly's mother called it. So, she was happily surprised to learn The Red Lion was a German pub.

Darkly walked into the Cha Cha Lounge no longer hungry and pleasantly buzzed. Toma was enjoying a pre-show drink at the bar. He wasn't alone. The elegant, middle-aged woman she'd seen at the venue in West Hollywood was with him. It seems she wasn't an undercover LAPD detective, after all. Unless Toma was one too? Toma leapt out of his chair and took Darkly's arm the moment he saw her.

"Darkly. You came."

"I said I would."

"I want you to meet my manager. Cassandra, this is Darkly Stewart."

Cassandra slid off a bar stool next to the tiki bar and reached out a hand with the longest fingers Darkly had ever seen. When Darkly accepted Cassandra's gesture, she found herself in a handshake she wasn't certain would end. Cassandra then placed her other hand over top of Darkly's, and the trap door was set.

"You are all Toma has spoken about today. I can see why," Cassandra said with a British accent.

Cassandra looked into Darkly's eyes as though she was examining her brain for imperfections.

Toma moved Darkly towards a whicker barstool, forcing Cassandra to let go of Darkly's hand. Darkly took a seat, and Toma signaled the bartender with three fingers. He plopped down three beers on the bar.

"Cassandra is our angel. There wouldn't be a band without her," explained Toma. "She's funded everything from the start."

"I know talent when I see it," Cassandra reassured Toma, feeding an only growing ego.

Darkly felt there was something telling about Cassandra in the word *see*. She didn't say *hear*. She wondered if Toma had to do something more than sing to get her to cut a cheque. That led Darkly to wonder if she was capable of simply enjoying anything, or did she need to analyze every situation, even on a forced few hours break from her job?

"Cassandra gave the band its name," Toma added.

"Why Moonkill?" Darkly asked.

Cassandra leaned in close to Darkly for the answer.

"You know, I read somewhere that murders are more likely to take place on a full moon night. After that, the name came about naturally. Toma kills it onstage, and it's almost always at night when he plays."

Cassandra laughed.

"The truth is, Darkly, I always have had a bit of a macabre nature, and Toma didn't have anything better up his sleeve."

Toma downed his beer.

"Well, I better get up there. Stick around till the very end. I've got a surprise for you. The drinks are on my tab tonight."

Cassandra winked at Darkly.

"By his tab, he means mine."

Darkly watched Toma walk under the hanging Day of the Dead décor up to the small stage and join his bandmates, who had been chilling at a booth table directly offstage.

The first set was good by most standards. Darkly appreciated the band's interesting takes on a couple of well-worn covers, like *Helter Skelter* sung as a ballad. But, it was the second set that found Darkly losing a sense of time, as she found herself sucked into a song about permanent loss. A path of perilous emotional detachment lay before the singer, with no hope for reconciliation with his own true nature. Darkly looked over at Cassandra, but the bar stool was now empty. On the bar, was a printed tab and several large bills.

Toma thanked the crowd for showing up and announced his last song. Darkly decided she would freshen up, and walked to the back of the room, where a vending machine held every kind of oddity. There were packs of trading cards from 1980s television hits, miniature versions of The Communist Manifesto, t-shirts with the club's skull logo on them, and candy cigarettes.

Darkly pushed the door open to the women's room and walked into a pentagram shaped room lined with a sink and black wooden panels. One of the wooden panels opened, and a woman with blue hair stepped out to wash her hands. Darkly pushed on another panel and found herself peering into a pink and black tiled cubicle with a toilet in the center of it. She stepped inside and locked the latch on the door.

Darkly's mind was suddenly racing back to chasing Marielle into the women's room at the Achoo club. What if all wasn't as it seemed in that women's room? Darkly heard Toma's voice hitting the final note of the song, as she re-emerged into the lounge.

Darkly found a fresh drink waiting for her at the bar. She picked up the bottle of beer and found a slip of paper underneath. There was a semblance of an address written on the paper. *Hollywood Sign parking, North Beachwood Drive. Meet me. You won't be disappointed. Toma.*

Darkly looked over at Toma, packing up his gear onstage. He made eye contact with her briefly, smiled, picked up his guitar case and headed out the back of the building. So, that was it, was it? A dare? Darkly felt her courage was being challenged. She could handle a twenty-something, spoiled kid from SoCal. She'd show up, thank him for a great evening, then get back in her car, drive to the little flat in Echo Park and resume her search for Marielle the next day.

Darkly winded her way up into the Hollywood Hills past homes that would cost a couple hundred thousand anywhere else, but were a million and above on Beachwood Drive. The road eventually dead-ended at a parking lot, over which the Hollywood sign loomed farther away than it appeared. The barrier was down, so Darkly couldn't drive inside, the way her GPS wanted her to. But, that was no matter. Toma was leaning against the barrier, smiling.

Darkly pulled the car over onto the side of the road and rolled down her window. Toma walked over and hung over the window, a little too close for comfort.

"I bet you thought I was hitting on you, didn't you? Expected to show up for a make-out session in the back of my car?"

"Something like that," Darkly answered.

"Well, I guess I'm not that corny. Truth is, I'm always wired after a show. I usually go for a run. With the moon as my running partner."

Toma let that sink in.

"But, I was thinking tonight, what about a hike? Everyone knows you have to do the sign at least once. It's iconic. What do you say?"

"It's late, Toma."

Darkly thought she caught a glare in Toma's eyes. Ever so briefly. A look that said *get out of the car, bitch*. But it passed.

"You're right," Toma admitted defeat. "Another time. When it's not so… dark. Good night, Darkly."

Toma tapped the top of Darkly's car and walked up ahead to what Darkly assumed was his own car.

"Goodnight, Toma. You were really great tonight," Darkly called out.

Toma opened the door to his car and turned to waive.

"By the way," Toma called back. "Marielle says hello."

Toma then slammed the door without getting in and jogged into the darkness at the end of the parking lot.

Darkly was dumbstruck. This had taken an unexpected turn. Now she remembered where she had seen Toma before. In Toronto, over a year ago, on the night she met Marielle. Tom, as he called himself then. A nerdy college kid looking to pop his cherry. And along came a lady werewolf with an insatiable sexual appetite. It was quite the transformation that encounter inspired in Tom.

"Goddammit."

Now Darkly had to follow him. She opened the glove compartment and pulled out her gun. She checked the cartridge for bullets out of habit.

"Shit," she said to herself. "They're not silver. It will have to do, Darkly."

She didn't want to kill the rock star wannabe, but she knew better to be prepared for the unexpected."

Darkly got out of the car and leapt into the darkness, her gun in hand.

At the end of the parking spaces, Darkly's eyesight had adjusted well enough to find the trailhead that led up to the Hollywood sign. She hit the dirt running, but then slowed to pace herself. It was a hell of an incline. She'd be out of breath in less than a quarter of a mile. She was sure Toma was counting on that. For all she knew, he'd already become a wolf.

Darkly estimated a mile to a mile and a half as the crow flies to get to the sign. But, the trail was bound to wind another mile or so. As she ascended, the lights of L.A. became a more expansive white, yellow and red glow below her. Every sound, a rustle in the brush, a twig snap, a flapping wind, an insect's call…they were all a wolf to Darkly.

Darkly checked her phone. She was forty-five minutes into the ascent, with about a hundred yards to go. She had no reception. She was completely alone. That's okay, she reassured herself. She'd been in such a place before.

On the final approach to the lit sign, Darkly sensed movement up ahead.

"Toma? Or is it Tom? I just want to talk."

"Talking wasn't what I had in mind," responded the disembodied voice.

Darkly jumped out of her skin. She whirled around. Toma's voice sounded like a whisper in her ear. There was nothing there. The next thing she heard was a woman's laughter. She recognized it immediately. It was Cassandra. Great. Two wolves.

Hope dashed into Darkly's brain in the form of Ennis's wolf whistle. She felt the breast pocket of her jacket and traced the outline of the whistle with her fingers. She pulled it out and popped it into her mouth and blew.

The hillside around her erupted in yelping and whining, and a fist slammed into her jaw, causing the whistle to go flying.

"That wasn't very nice," complained Toma in a theatrical voice. Then he was gone again.

Darkly fell to the ground and felt around frantically for the whistle. It was Cassandra who served the next volley.

"Darkly Stewart. The little Mountie girl who wishes she was wolf. We know all about you."

The next thing Darkly knew, Cassandra's impossibly long fingers were tangled up in her hair and dragging her to her feet. Darkly hit out, as she was trained, and Cassandra blocked the move. Strike and parry followed again and again. Darkly was dealing with no amateur. Someone who at the very least had the money to hire a fight instructor.

Darkly and Cassandra took a step back from one another. Toma stepped out of the brush to join Cassandra. He was naked.

"They're luxury labels. No point in ruining them," said Toma, off Darkly's look.

The brush around Darkly shook with movement. She pulled her gun from her belt and pointed it into the dark, then at Cassandra and Toma.

"Don't worry, darling. They're not going to kill you," Cassandra assured Darkly.

"I am," Toma added.

"His first kill. Hand-picked by me."

That explained why Darkly had not tasted murder in her mouth when she became reacquainted with Tom. Now, she was damn curious.

"Who killed the scoutmaster? Marielle?" Darkly finally spoke.

"His band. I've indoctrinated them all," Cassandra explained. "But, I knew it needed to be someone special for my special pet."

Toma's band circled the small party in wolf form. Cassandra reached out to grab Toma's hard cock.

"Look how excited he is. He can't wait."

Then Toma began to change. Darkly watched in horror as his face elongated, his back snapped, and a hump thrust out of his back.

"When Marielle spilled the beans," Cassandra continued, "I knew we'd found his ideal prey. The poor little wolf girl, Darkly. Only, she's not a wolf at all. She's defective. A reject."

Toma collapsed to the dirt on all fours, his face now more wolf than human. He looked up at Darkly, hunger in his eyes.

"Almost there," Cassandra said with glee. "Get ready, get set. Go!"

Toma, now almost all wolf except for a couple of ears that looked like they belonged on one of Santa's demented elves, inched forward.

At that very moment, a shrill croak filled the air, and a raven plunged down between Toma and Darkly. It pecked at the dirt on the trail and flung Darkly's lost whistle, now found, up into the air with its beak. Darkly raced forward, diving for the whistle, as Toma leapt into the air to snap his jaws at the raven, that was now escaping into the black night from whence it appeared. Missing its target, Toma landed a foot from Darkly, as she raised the whistle to her mouth. She could feel his hot breath on her face.

Darkly blew into the metal hole and released the longest breath she had ever inhaled. The result was as though Toma had slammed into a brick wall. He turned his head to bury his snout under his paws. Darkly leveled her gun at Cassandra and fired. Cassandra dove for the brush the second she saw Darkly point the gun at her. The gunshots echoed across the hills, and dogs everywhere began barking.

As for Toma and his band of wolves, they turned in circles and howled in agony. When Darkly took a breath, Toma and the other wolves recovered and leapt for her. Toma's claw ripped through her shoe and dug into her flesh, as she blew the whistle again with all her might. At that point, each wolf turned tail and ran down the hill, instinctually knowing only distance could silence the pain.

Darkly turned in circles, leveling her gun at every imagined attack. Cassandra was still out there. The wolves would come back. Think, Darkly, think, she thought. It was half an hour minimum down the hill. What was above her? There's a radio tower and a bunker of some sort. Maybe there was someone on duty. If she was lucky, there was someone. Maybe that raven would return and carry her out of this place. How crazy was that bird?

Darkly ran for the sign and climbed the steep incline behind it. She needed to slip her gun under her belt, as it took both hands to climb. She thrust her nails into the dirt and scrambled up the hill as fast as she may have done on two legs. Maybe she was suited to a life on all fours, after all. The whistle remained in Darkly's mouth, and every exhale emitted the silent torture. In this instance, it was better than a firearm.

Twenty minutes later, Darkly pulled herself up over the top and returned to her feet to jog towards a bunker under a red and white radio tower. She propelled herself onto the chain link fence that encircled the bunker, climbed to the top and dropped down on the other side. There was a pickup truck parked outside the door to the bunker. She raced past it to bang on the door. No answer. Her ears picked up the sound of automobile shocks squeaking. The noise a truck makes bouncing down a bumpy road. Darkly looked back to see the truck shaking slightly.

She walked up to the truck and peered through the fogged-up driver's side window. A naked foot hit the window and smudged the condensation. Then came the unmistakable accelerated moans of finishing the job. The truck stopped moving, and Darkly knocked on the window. Commotion replaced ecstasy in the cab.

"What the fuck?" a man's voice yelled.

The window rolled down as fast as a hand-cranked window could go. A pudgy nondescript sort of guy glared back at her, pulling on his shirt.

"Where did you come from?" He asked angrily.

Darkly looked past the guy to the naked girl sinking into the other corner of the cab. It was Marielle. Darkly grabbed the handle to the driver's door and yanked it open. The guy grabbed the inside of the door and tried to pull it shut again. But, Marielle took advantage of the opportunity to kick the guy in the head and push him out of the door.

Darkly broke his fall, taking all his weight. In the time it took her to push him off, Marielle had slid behind the wheel and started the engine. She threw the gearshift into reverse and gunned the accelerator. Marielle backed the truck at full speed through the chain link gate and undertook a three-point turn, during which time Darkly managed to catch up with the truck. She leapt into the bed of the pickup, as Marielle sped off, now facing the right direction.

Darkly looked behind her to see a pack of wolves entering the now unprotected compound. She watched in horror as Marielle's john ran for the door to the compound. He felt his naked ass, where his pockets should have been. The situation was hopeless. Darkly blew on the whistle that was firmly clenched in her teeth, but Marielle had put too much distance between the wolves and them for it to be anything more than an annoyance. She pulled her gun and took aim, as two wolves latched on to the man's arms. They were going to literally rip him apart. He was going to face the worst possible death imaginable.

The truck jolted and swerved. Darkly understood that Marielle was trying to throw her out of the truck. She only had the opportunity to take one shot before the line of shot would disappear, as they careened down the Hollywood Hills. She took it. The bullet hit the guy who was in the wrong place at the wrong time square between the eyes. He wouldn't feel any more pain. The beauty of it, of course, is that he would wake up in the morgue ready to tackle a brave new chapter in his life. Thanks to Marielle. The gunshot also scattered the attacking wolves.

Darkly looked back at the woman she had been hunting. What she saw instead of a human form was a wolf leaping out of the passenger window. The truck was driverless and drifted off to the right. The vehicle hit the earth ridge at the side of the dirt road and was airborne. Darkly knew it would come crashing down on the forty-five-degree angle of the hill and begin a tumble that would result in her broken neck at best. She wasn't willing to bet that she would wake up in the morgue fully repaired. So, she leapt out of the bed of the truck, hit the ground and rolled.

She got up as quickly as a paratrooper and ran down the road that led back to civilization. Five seconds later, she heard the truck explode. Ten seconds after that, she heard the first police siren. It was then Darkly realized she had lost the whistle for good.

CHAPTER FOURTEEN

Darkly poured herself a shot of tequila from the bottle she found in the freezer of her new home. There were so many questions she needed answers to. Who was Cassandra, really? Did that raven follow here thousands of miles, or were all ravens her personal protectors now? How did Marielle fit into all of this? And where the hell was Buck?

Darkly had been right about the hooker hunch, and she had another hunch. She remembered hearing about a speakeasy in New Orleans. The entrance was through a women's toilet stall of a law-abidingly dry restaurant. With that thought, she gathered up her things and got the hell out of the Echo Park flat. She placed a text message, *I've been compromised*, and cautiously walked to her double-parked car. Toma knew where she was staying, so there was no coming back. She was homeless for the time being, and whistle-less. She wasn't about to return to the Hollywood sign to find that needle in a haystack.

It was well after midnight now, but she suspected Achoo was still going strong. She made her way to the club and entered without any hassle from a bouncer who was now drinking at the bar himself. The club was winding down, with only a handful of millennials, what looked like the remnants of a bachelorette party, left on the dancefloor. One of the dancers was covered in a disintegrating toilet tissue wedding dress. Darkly ordered a drink and stood by a Copa table close to the toilets. After a couple of sips, she abandoned her drink and walked down the hallway to the women's room.

Inside, Darkly was greeted with the sound of retching from one of the stalls. Darkly walked past and looked out the window. To the left, along the brick wall was exactly what Darkly was looking for. When she looked to the right, there was a smooth brick wall. But, to the left, the wall pushed out to form a narrow box of bricks about seven feet tall. Anyone would think it an accommodation in the structure for plumbing. Maybe that's all it was. Or maybe it was something more.

Darkly pulled her head back inside and pushed the door of the stall closest to the window open. She stepped inside and locked the door behind her. She could hear the girl a couple of stalls away dry heaving. Good. If someone else came in, they'd be distracted by that. Darkly examined the subway tiles that lined the inside of the outside wall and the load bearing wall behind the toilet. Amongst the white tiles, was the occasional black one. She pushed on the black tiles. They didn't give. She traced the grouting between the tiles, looking for imperfections, but found none.

The toilet then beckoned Darkly. She realized she hadn't gone to the bathroom for hours, and the drink she ordered had prompted some urgency. As she sat, she examined the floor. It was concrete. There were no exceptional cracks that suggested a trap door. She got up and examined the wall behind the cistern. The flush mechanism was not part of the toilet. It was built into the wall. She flushed. All the normal things happened. She stood back and thought. She then ran her fingers over the flush again and lifted up, instead of pushing down. There was a distinctive click beside her, the kind of click when something unlocks.

Darkly turned to the outside wall again and placed both of her hands against it and pushed. The entire wall below the top of the stall slid back over a hole in the floor. She held her phone over the hole, lighting a stairwell. Darkly didn't like the look of this. She knew what happened to women in horror films who descend stairs leading to the bowels of a building in the middle of the night.

She had no choice. She'd signed up for this crusade. Turning back now meant chaos for the world she may not have been born into, but had come to be quite fond of. The threat had to be contained, and the wolves of Wolf Woods saved from the societal backlash and slaughter Buck was too naïve or delusional to see coming. This was her task, even if it is was to become her life's work.

Darkly descended the stairs until she reached a basement level. Directly ahead of the last step, was a black-out curtain. She felt silently for the opening in the curtain and, when she found it, took a deep breath and pulled it ever so slightly apart to see what she could see inside. Firelight greeted her.

Through the curtain, was a world of comfort. There were a couple of sofas and a fireplace with a roaring fire. The walls were covered in wood paneling from the 1970s. The carpet was shag. This was a disco king's man cave before they became the necessary third room in any house purchase.

There was a bar in one corner with a refrigerator and sink, and a cathode ray tube television on a rolling cart. There was a closed door in the middle of one of the four walls. Darkly walked toward the fireplace. When she got to the sofa, she could see over it onto the floor. There, on a faux bearskin rug, was Marielle's nude figure, fast asleep. She was clearly exhausted from the night's activities.

"Mummy?"

Darkly whirled around and drew her gun on a toddler boy rubbing his eyes and then quickly hid the weapon behind her back. Marielle stirred, and Darkly held her finger to her lips.

"Shh. I'm a friend of your Mommy's. Let's not wake her up. Come on, back to bed."

Darkly ushered the toddler back through the now open door. Inside the child's room, was a cot, a diaper changing table, plastic bins of toys and clothes, and a nightlight. Darkly put the little boy on the cot and covered him with blankets. He rolled over and went back to sleep, clearly exhausted himself.

At that, Darkly heard the cocking of a shotgun hammer behind her and Marielle's voice.

"Step away from my son."

Darkly raised her hands in the air.

"Slowly."

"I'll go as slow as you want," replied Darkly, backing up from the child.

Marielle backed out of the room, and Darkly followed her out backwards.

"Shut the door. Quietly," commanded Marielle.

Darkly did so.

"Now," continued Marielle, "put your gun on the floor and step away from it."

Darkly did as she was ordered once again.

"Sit. But keep your hands where I can see them."

Darkly sat on the sofa, and Marielle picked up the gun.

"You came here to kill us. Kill an innocent child. My baby."

Marielle was growing emotional. That made her even more dangerous, worried Darkly.

"What? Take a look in the clip. They aren't silver bullets. I came to find you and bring you home. What made you think I was going to kill you?"

"Because you tried to kill us in Wolf Woods. Buck saw the Mountie, your friend, shoot Wyatt. He would have shot the both of us, too, if we hadn't gotten away. You brought him to kill us. And now you're hunting us. Buck warned me this would happen. I came here so me and my son could stop hiding. I promised myself I wouldn't hide anymore. After I kill you, my son will have a normal life. I trusted you."

Marielle was in tears now.

"And you still can trust me, Marielle. Wyatt isn't dead. My friend didn't kill anyone. He came to Wolf Woods because he knew I was in trouble. It was all a big mistake."

"Prove it," challenged Marielle.

"I can prove it. Just let me remove my phone. I'll call Wyatt right now. You can speak with him. The Mountie who shot him. By accident, Marielle. Wyatt is staying with him. The Mountie is keeping his secret and mine. There's nothing to fear from us. I swear to you. Just let me call Wyatt. You can see him."

Marielle waved her gun, and Darkly lowered her hands slowly.

"Just one hand," Marielle said excitedly.

Darkly's left hand shot back up, and she reassured Marielle.

"Okay. No problem."

With her right hand, Darkly removed her phone and dialed Ennis's number. She chose the video option. It took quite a few rings, but Ennis finally picked up.

"Darkly?"

"Uncle Ennis."

"Should you be calling me? Someone might be listening in. Are you alright?"

"I'm fine, Ennis. I need to speak with Wyatt. It's very important. Life or death. My life."

Darkly held the phone up to take in the image of Marielle holding the shotgun.

"I see, Darkly. I'll go get him. He's chopping wood."

Ennis set his phone down, and Darkly tried to engage Marielle in logical conversation.

"You found your son's father. He's a little different from how I remember him. I'd say you're better matched now."

"He was supposed to kill you tonight, so his son would be safe from the wolf killer forever. He's a good man."

"I'm sure," said Darkly sarcastically.

"He is, Darkly."

"Did he tell you to sell your body?"

Marielle was silent for a few moments. Darkly saw shame in her face.

"Toma says it's our duty. It's what Buck wanted. The more people we turn, the safer we'll be."

"That doesn't sound like Buck to me," Darkly countered. "He wanted families of wolves to colonize the world outside of Wolf Woods, for you to find your mate and raise children with that mate. Those children would choose their mates, and so on. Wolf begat wolf. Slow but effective."

Darkly was putting a positive spin on things. She knew full well that one-night-stands were part of the plan. But, Buck would never have wanted those under his care to degrade themselves. Marielle was a slave to Toma. Or was she a slave to Cassandra?

"You don't know anything, Darkly."

"Darkly?"

It was Wyatt's voice.

"Wyatt?" Marielle answered.

Marielle lowered the shotgun and rushed to the phone, which Darkly handed to her.

"You were dead," said Marielle with confidence.

"It wasn't a silver bullet. I'm okay. And I remember more of who and what I was. But, it's like watching a movie about someone else. I don't recognize the man as me. I've been given a second chance, Marielle. Think about it. If Darkly didn't kill me, she's not going to kill you. But, if you don't come home, eventually someone will kill you, once they figure out what you are. Come home, Marielle."

With that, Wyatt passed the phone to Ennis.

"Darkly, Wyatt thinks he's found the right location to start again. More remote, but with woods for hunting, grazing land and an unending water supply. I've decided I'd like to be one of the founders of the new Wolf Woods. A chance to be useful again. It's my choice. And I've spoken with a few others from my tribe looking for a new start."

"I understand," Darkly answered, not at all surprised by what she heard.

"Ennis out."

And with that sign-off, the screen went black. Uncle Ennis's words struck a chord with Darkly. *My choice*, he said. She wanted to bring Marielle back to Canada for the safety of the world, but also for hers and her son's safety. Yet, who was she to force her will upon any other person? She suddenly found clarity. Her mission was not to hunt and impose, but to track and persuade.

"Marielle, if you want me to walk out of here and leave you and your son and never come back, I will. But, think about it. In a community of wolves, your son will always be protected. Someone will always have his back. Here, the chances of him growing old without being killed, well, ask yourself how realistic you think that is."

Marielle's voice wavered in certainty when she replied.

"I have Toma. We're a family."

"Marielle, I think we both know that Toma is under Cassandra's control. You're the strong one. He'll do whatever he's told. You need to be stronger than her."

Marielle leaned the shotgun against the wall and took a seat on the sofa next to Darkly.

"She owns this place," Marielle said with a wave of her hand. "Cassandra. I found Toma playing dives in Toronto. He was good. He'd survived the change without me. It had given him confidence, he told me, that he didn't have before. So, we came south to where all dreams come true."

"That's when you met Cassandra?" Darkly asked.

"Yes. She came to one of his shows. Told him he had talent. He likes flattery, and he likes to brag. It's his weakness."

"That's a lot of men, Marielle, werewolf or not."

Marielle looked down at herself and realized she was still naked. "I'm still…"

She grabbed a blanket off the back of the sofa and wrapped herself in it.

"He was with her the night our son was born. Paying her for the promise to make him a star. She's one of us now."

Marielle looked into the fire for a few seconds before finishing her thought.

"It's selfish not to share, he told me."

"Do you know where they are now?" Darkly asked, glancing at the stairwell that led up to the women's toilets.

Marielle reached out and touched Darkly's fingers.

"His band was going to play the Cha Cha Lounge, then he was going to stop you from hurting us. Permanently. He wanted me nearby to see the body for myself, so I wouldn't be scared anymore. Then, Cassandra was taking him and the band to play in London. A private party."

"It's too late to fly. They're not going anywhere till morning."

"Did I mention she's an heiress? She owns her own plane, Darkly."

Darkly promised she would bring Toma back to Marielle. Her son would have a father. In return, Marielle promised to return to the woods. Darkly knew how she would achieve this. The night had been a moment of truth. She had come to L.A. with the objective of bringing wolves home. She now knew that objective must change. For wolves like Cassandra, who got her highs from death, there could be no redemption. If she lived, she would continue to corrupt the other wolves around her.

So, Darkly found herself stepping into a 24/7 gun shop and purchasing five silver bullets. She had promised to bring back

Toma. But, if she had to, she would kill the bandmates along with Cassandra. They had all taken innocent lives. At least she assumed Cassandra had. The only one who was still relatively pure was Toma. For Marielle's sake, Darkly hoped he remained so.

After acquiring the bullets that meant permanent death, Darkly drove to Burbank and parked her car a half mile from the end of the Bob Hope Airport runway. She crossed one wide ditch and climbed two chain link fences before reaching the end of the runway. She kept to the shadows at the edge of the runway and made her way to a series of hangers by the airport's terminal. The airport was now closed to commercial airliner takeoffs and landings. If it was closed to private takeoffs, as well, Darkly was certain Cassandra would have bought her way around the rule.

A sliver of light appeared on one of the hangers and grew wider. A door was opening. Once fully open, Darkly watched the nose of a small passenger jet emerge. The plane had begun its taxi to the runway. Darkly pulled a clip from her pocket and inserted silver bullets into the clip. She loaded the clip into her gun, left the shadows behind and ran for the plane.

At the sound of the engines on the plane powering down, Darkly ducked behind a baggage cart left on the tarmac. She climbed on and peered through the rain flaps of the cart cover. The door to the plane opened, and steps lowered to the ground. A woman in a flight attendant's uniform stepped out and looked in Darkly's direction.

Darkly ducked for cover, and it was then that she first heard the quiet car behind her. The luxury electric automobile rushed past the baggage cart and pulled up next to the flight attendant. Cassandra got out of the car first, followed by Toma and the band. It was now or never. There was no time for hesitation. Darkly needed to take Cassandra out.

So, the Mountie sprang into action. She leapt from the cart and ran, her gun in her hand ready to fire. Cassandra didn't see her. Neither did the band. But the flight attendant did, and she was no mere stewardess. She turned and reached into the plane, withdrawing a semi-automatic weapon. Darkly fired her first shot at Cassandra and missed. The flight attendant got in the next shot when she sprayed the ground in front of Darkly, as Cassandra and the band hurried onboard. Darkly stopped.

The flight attendant backed up onto the plane and yelled something Darkly couldn't hear at the car that had dropped the travelers off. The plane was moving before the door to the plane was fully shut. Darkly began running again. At that point, the car turned around and sped towards Darkly. There was nowhere for her to run and escape in time. She lowered her gun at the car's windshield and fired. The bullet hit the top of the glass, which did not shatter. The car kept coming. Darkly fired again. The bullet embedded itself in the windshield, but again, it did not shatter. It was a fucking bullet-proof car. Darkly had two bullets left, and the car was ten seconds from mowing her down.

That's when she did something crazy. She started running again. Head on at the car. It was a Hail Mary. Two seconds before impact, Darkly dove to the right and rolled up into a sitting position as the car missed her by inches. She fired both shots into the rear passenger side tire. It blew. Fortunately for her, the tires weren't bullet-proof.

The driver of the car lost control, and the vehicle skidded off the tarmac and into a ditch. By the time the emergency personnel emerged from the terminal, Darkly had disappeared once again into the shadows. She had failed again.

CHAPTER FIFTEEN

Darkly stopped into a Mexican bar to wind down. It had been one hell of a night. She ordered a shot of bourbon with a Mexican beer chaser. What was the next step? She had to come up with a plan quickly that would snatch hope from the jaws of disaster.

Marielle needed to leave Los Angeles before she turned anyone else. The girl's sexual appetite was bound to get the better of her with Toma not around. Darkly needed to get to London and stop Cassandra. By the end of her beer, she knew the next steps.

It took some explaining to Marielle, but Darkly convinced her that she would chase Toma around the world to bring him back if that's what it took. Right now, she needed to get Marielle and her son to a place where they would be safe and provided for. A place where Marielle would never again need to leave her son asleep alone in a basement without windows. So, they packed up Darkly's car with clothing and supplies and left Los Angeles. It would be a two-day drive north. When the threesome stopped for their first bathroom and food break, Darkly made a call to

Vincetti. There was one loose end in Los Angeles that needed taking care of.

The undercover agent who *greeted* Darkly at LAX, when she had arrived in Los Angeles, walked through the hospital corridor in surgeon's scrubs and attracted no suspicion when he stepped into the elevator and selected the basement level. He entered the unattended morgue and examined a chart as though it was a common ritual for him. Perhaps it was.

The agent then walked to a wall of body fridges and opened the right one. He pulled the drawer out that held the body of the man Darkly had shot in the head. He then inserted the stethoscope around his neck into his ears and placed the chest piece over the man's heart. If anyone had witnessed the agent's face, they would have sworn it turned a couple shades lighter at that moment. But, he kept his composure, removed a syringe from his pocket and injected a clear liquid into the man's chest.

Fifteen minutes later, the agent rolled a gurney out one of the back doors of the hospital, and up to the open doors of a white, unmarked van. Inside, was a metal casket. The kind used to transport a body across international borders.

Marielle and her son were sleeping when Darkly pulled up to the Canadian border two and a half days after leaving Los Angeles. It was lunchtime, and the queue of cars crossing the border was long. Darkly made a call.

"RCMP Constable Darkly Stewart. Peace Arch Crossing. License Plate number 5UMH717. California."

That was all Darkly said, and then hung up. Forty-five minutes later, Darkly was five cars behind the lead car. A custom's official walked down the queue of cars and nodded at Darkly. He pointed over to a road that went around the customs checkpoints. Darkly pulled out of the line and followed the road to an unmarked building the size of a taco stand. She parked in front of it and turned off the engine.

At that point, another customs officer stepped out of the building and approached Darkly's car. She rolled down the window, and the officer held out a smartphone at eye level.

"Hold still please," he instructed Darkly.

A red light passed across Darkly's eyes, and then the smartphone beeped. The officer studied the results.

"You're free to go, constable."

That was it. The officer barely glanced at Marielle, who was holding a puppy in the back seat. Back on the road, Darkly didn't stop again until the outskirts of Whistler. They pulled into a motor inn and got adjoining rooms. One bed for Darkly, and one for Marielle and her boy.

Darkly had learned on the road trip that Marielle had named her son Neb. After the king who had found redemption. An act of hope, Darkly thought. She had kept Neb occupied with sing-alongs and various stuffed animals she bought for him along the route. But, Darkly also had time to contemplate her impossible mission and how the playing field was not exactly level. Despite that fact, tomorrow, Ennis would arrive to take Marielle and Neb home with him, and Darkly would fly on to London. This was her life from now until she dropped dead.

Darkly fiddled with the vent control above her window seat on the Boeing 747. She couldn't seem to get comfortable. The temperature had been rising steadily since takeoff and through the evening meal. Now, most of the plane's passengers slept around her. She couldn't understand how the man in the middle seat next to hers was wrapped tightly in a blanket. Darkly had removed her bra and now pulled at the t-shirt that was sticking to her sweaty body.

She lifted the window shade and looked out at a bright moon that cast its glow on the blanket of clouds below the plane. It hurt

Darkly's eyes. And she had a pounding headache. That was it. She needed to splash some water on her body, or throw-up, or pull her hair out. One thing she couldn't do was sit still any longer. So, Darkly pushed her way past the two grunting passengers to her left and moved quickly down the aisle.

The flight attendant in the back galley gave Darkly a sympathetic, knowing look, as she slipped into the unoccupied lavatory. Darkly was feeling dizzy now, as she plopped down on the toilet. She hung her head down between her legs and breathed deeply. One breath. Two breaths. She tried to slow her racing heart by sheer will. It wasn't working.

Darkly got up and put her mouth under the faucet to lap up water. My God, she thought, she had never been so thirsty. She rubbed her itchy eyes and looked up into the mirror. They were bloodshot, and the whites of her eyes had turned yellow and murky. Darkly pulled at the bags under eyes, and then suddenly had to rinse her hands with cold water. They felt like they were on fire. Red blisters were rising from under the skin.

Next, Darkly's fingernails began growing before her eyes. They were like daggers shooting out from deep within her skin. They had always been a challenge for Darkly to keep under control, but had never grown at such a speed before. With her elongated hands, Darkly grasped at her neck. She couldn't breathe. She gasped, her lips groping at air they could not capture. Then, she watched her entire jaw jut forward in an agonizing stretch. Darkly collapsed to the floor and kicked at the door, needing space.

"Miss? Miss? Are you alright?"

The flight attendant on the other side of the door pulled at the door handle, while Darkly pleaded with inhuman eyes for the woman not to open the door.

Marielle shook Darkly.

"Are you alright? Darkly?"

Darkly inhaled deeply. She'd been holding her breath in her sleep and thrashing around in the sheets, which were now twisted around her body like a straightjacket.

"I'm okay. Just a really weird dream."

Marielle turned on the light and helped Darkly unwrap herself. She shut the door to the adjoining room, so that Neb wouldn't wake up. Darkly noticed Marielle was wearing something she'd likely worn for Toma's benefit. The nighty hung short, not covering the bottom of Marielle's, well, bottom. She wasn't wearing any panties. It inspired desire. Darkly's lust inspired thoughts on a solution that, if it worked, would give her a leg up in London.

Darkly had been curious before. She had wondered about the sensations men experienced during sex. She had contemplated acting on her curiosity in the past, but never followed through. Now, she wondered if she made love with Marielle, if that would be enough to undo the cure that stopped her from becoming what her DNA said she should be. Darkly was staring at the faint blue lines on her lower neck. But, her hand had moved under the sheet down to between her legs. Marielle took notice.

Marielle looked down at her own faint spider veins and sat down on the bed next to Darkly. She reached out and ran her fingertip along Darkly's neck.

"They'll never go away completely," Marielle said, answering Darkly's unspoken question.

Marielle traced the veins, moving her finger down below Darkly's neck and over one of her breasts. She then lifted her nighty up over her head and placed Darkly's free hand on her own neck and guided the hand down over her breasts, then her stomach, and then to her inner thigh.

Darkly woke up late. It was after 8am. The drive and then Marielle had worn her out. She looked next to her at the empty place on the bed. She got up and pressed her ear to the door that led to the adjoining room. No peep, so she opened the door just a crack and looked in. The room was empty.

"Fuck," said Darkly out loud.

Marielle had done a runner. How could Darkly have been so stupid? So close, and she'd dropped her guard at the last moment. She should have had Ennis meet them at the border to handle the trade-off. Darkly threw her clothes on and flung open the door to the outside to see Marielle standing there with Neb and two Styrofoam cups.

"I thought you might need some coffee," Marielle said coyly.

Later that morning, on the side of the Trans-Canada Highway, Darkly said goodbye to Marielle and Neb, but not before promising again to bring father and lover back to them.

The next part of the plan was for Darkly to park the car at the Vancouver long-term parking lot, throw the keys away and purchase a ticket for London. But, after last night – both the dream and the tryst – Darkly had to adjust the plan. She boarded a flight to Toronto. Twenty-Four hours after arriving back where she started, she was speaking to Vincetti face-to-face, while she was chained to a tree in the acres of wood behind her sergeant's home.

Darkly looked down at the shackles that tightly grasped her feet and the zip ties that bound her wrists together. Vincetti, meanwhile, opened a folding lawn chair and took a seat just out of reach of Darkly.

"Oh," remembered Vincetti.

He got up and wrapped a blanket around Darkly.

"Thank you," she said. "For everything."

"How long?" asked Vincetti.

"Anytime now."

Two hours later and Vincetti was drifting off. Two hours after that, and Darkly was shivering uncontrollably from the cold. Vincetti gave her the second blanket he had been using to keep warm. An hour after that, and Vincetti had reached his limit.

"Darkly. This isn't happening. We're going to catch hypothermia. It's time to go in."

"Okay," replied Darkly through chattering teeth.

Vincetti released Darkly, and they both returned to his home, a fireplace, and a bottle of wine.

"I guess I really am cured," said Darkly glumly.

"Isn't that a good thing, Darkly?"

"I don't know."

With that, Darkly fell asleep on Vincetti's sofa and dreamt of Buck. Where the hell was he? He wasn't in L.A. Marielle didn't know where he had disappeared to. He could be anywhere in the world. Wherever he was, did he dream of her?

Vincetti agreed to chain Darkly up for three more nights. Perhaps with Darkly, there was a delay in the transformation. Buck had told her she was special. She was a direct descendant of the one who had achieved redemption. But, nothing was achieved except for Darkly needing the tip of one of her small toes removed because of frostbite.

CHAPTER SIXTEEN

Buck had come close to showing up at Darkly's front door. He told Marielle that the Mountie may be *one of them*, but she had chosen a different path. She was dangerous and detrimental to the mission that lay before them. She would kill Marielle's new son if given the chance, just as she had Wyatt killed. She may not like it, but Darkly would perform what she thought was her duty to protect.

The truth was a little different. Buck was thinking of Darkly's best interests. She had a life she did not need to give up for his or anyone's else's sake. Not now that Wolf Woods had been abandoned. The process of transforming the world was a long one. It would be well after Buck's remaining years that the effects would be noticeable across the world and irreversible.

But, Buck did love Darkly. There was a connection with her he had never felt with any other woman. So, he went to her to tell her how he felt. To thank her for coming back to Wolf Woods, when she did not have to, and to tell her not to worry that chaos was coming. There was a plan for order. An old authority was returning to the world of wolves.

When the sheriff of no town looked inside the window of Darkly's flat, he saw her and Vincetti groping one another on her sofa. She had already moved on. It was not what he wanted to see, but it was what he needed to see.

Now, Buck stood on Hampstead Heath in north London, ready to oversee the coronation of a new Queen of Wolves. Every new wolf from this night forward would know they were part of a complex society. A community of laws and traditions. The new queen would be crowned where every queen for the last millennium had been crowned. Europe. The moon was setting over the heath, when Geraldine stepped forward and lowered the robe she was wearing to her waist. Gus walked up behind her and took the robe, removing it fully. He stepped away, and Geraldine knelt on the grass. Buck stepped forward, and Geraldine raised her arms into the air. Buck reached into a black satchel on the ground and pulled out two leather gloves. He reached back in with the gloves on and pulled out a shirt of metal rings. Silver rings. He lifted the shirt above Geraldine and let it fall over her arms and torso.

"Do you accept the weight and burden of your office freely?" Buck asked Geraldine.

From the immediate contact of all that silver to flesh, Geraldine shuddered and collapsed to the ground. Her mouth opened in shock, and she tried to find the words to answer, but could not. Buck put his mouth to Geraldine's ear and repeated the question.

"Do you accept the weight and burden of your office freely?"

"Yes-s," Geraldine barely managed.

Buck stood again and nodded at Gus, who joined him by Geraldine's side. They both pulled her to her feet and held her hands tightly. They helped her walk to a large oak tree nearby. Her steps were like those of a stroke victim learning to walk again. She called out to no one in muffled wails. The two men let her loose, and Geraldine reached out to steady herself against the tree trunk.

"Three times round, a queen is bound. Wisdom, Justice and Sacrifice," Buck instructed.

Geraldine steadied herself and began her walk around the tree. She made it all the way around the trunk and then stopped to take several deep breaths.

"God has granted you wisdom," proclaimed Gus.

Geraldine began her second walk around the wide tree trunk. Halfway around, she faltered and fell to her knees. Gus moved to support her.

"No," ordered Buck. "She has to do it on her own."

Geraldine waved Gus away and dug her nails into the tree bark to pull herself to her feet. She finished the second revolution.

"The wisdom to deliver justice," continued Buck.

Geraldine nodded at Buck and began her third and final trek. She limped and clung to the tree for dear life. She almost passed out, but shook it off. If she had collapsed then and lost consciousness, then the trial could not continue. Nor would she be granted a second attempt.

Her mouth and hands were shaking when she finished the third march around the tree. Now, it was Geraldine's turn to speak.

"I sacrifice my life to duty," Geraldine declared through chattering teeth.

No more would Geraldine be allowed to make babies. Well, that was the official line it was hoped she would uphold. She was mother to the wellbeing of her subjects. With that, Geraldine's eyes rolled into the back of her head, and she lost all sense of place and time. Buck removed the shirt of silver chains from Geraldine's body. Where they had touched her skin, were now rings of blood. These rings, in the morning, would become the hallmark of royalty. They would transform into pale blue circles, left behind by the world's purest silver, that would reveal Geraldine to her people wherever she went.

Heathrow was swarming with people. It never mattered what time of year it was. London was one of the world's top destinations. As the saying went, whatever you were looking for in the world...in London, you would find it. The never-ending stream of people moving like a giant living organism for the London Underground escalators was something Darkly did not join. Vincetti had arranged a jump seat on a military transport.

Her hotel in economical Paddington came with a springy mattress, a bathroom that meant pressing your body into the wall to close the door, all in order to get to the toilet. But, at least there was a full English breakfast included. No cheese Danish and a weak coffee, like home. There was strong tea, unsettlingly large sausages, or bangers, eggs, mushrooms, beans, tomatoes and both fried and toasted bread.

The tourists would arrive on their buses-in-the-air and push through the day and go to bed early, so that they were adjusted to the time difference by day two. For Darkly, it worked out perfectly that she could sleep through the first day and begin her hunt at night, when results were most often achieved.

Vincetti looked into Cassandra's flight. It had landed at London's Luton Airport and appeared to still be there. Five American nationals had deplaned. Through his connections at Britain's Home Office, Vincetti could inform Darkly they were still in the UK, but not where.

Katty Sandra Schleswig-Holst, the woman who owned the aircraft, was indeed an heiress. Never married, no children, she was the only child of a man who invented components of a drill that made offshore oil-drilling possible and, thus, profitable. Katty's mother died from cancer when her daughter was still a toddler. The girl was shipped off to England at eleven to be educated and did not leave, save for Christmas holidays and brief summer sojourns with her father in Europe. At the London School of Economics, she learned what it took to succeed at business on an international stage. Well, those details explained the British accent.

What Vincetti's report did not reveal was that Cassandra, as she had been known to her friends since she was a child, had sold her father's company and deposited the proceeds from the sale into a Swizz bank account. Even the family mansion in Louisiana had been sold. All of this had taken place six months ago.

Also six months before Darkly met her, Cassandra had broken off communication with even her closest of friends. When they called, they got a voice message saying that Cassandra had gone off to find her true self. Darkly learned all of this easily enough online. A Vanity Fair columnist had even mentioned the strange affair of the social butterfly who had become the high society version of a backpacker, hopping from one dingy hotel to the next. The debutante who had never settled down had uncharacteristically switched to rough trade in the bedroom department. In the end, it was assumed that Cassandra was yet another wealth hoarder to succumb to the disease of a weak grip...not able to hold on tightly enough to one's sanity.

If she had been born a man, such a state of mind would have meant she was now only good for a U.S. senate run. Or, if lack of intelligence accompanied the midlife crisis, the formation of a committee to explore a run for President would be the surer bet. But, as Cassandra was very much a woman, she chose to become a werewolf and bring chaos to the stifling societal structure she had been born into.

There was more Darkly needed to know about Cassandra. She had brought Toma and his band to London to perform at a private party. Why? What did Cassandra have to gain from managing a band? Was it possible that she knew the hosts of the party well? Were they friends or, perhaps, people Cassandra harbored a secret grudge towards? Was Cassandra going to do something like reveal her new self at the party?

My God, thought Darkly. What if this party was a coming out? Her whole life, Cassandra had lived in the shadow of her late father. An inventor, genius, state governor before his wife's death. What if this was the way she was to leave her mark? To outshine dad? Darkly would bet her salary that when Cassandra learned from Marielle the plan to spread werewolfism around the world, the heiress saw the opportunity to become the glamourous face of a new world order. Their queen, if you will.

Darkly needed to figure out quickly who Cassandra knew in London, and which one of them was throwing a party. And how did she know it had already not taken place? There were no wolf mugs on the morning covers of the tabloids. That was a hopeful sign.

Geraldine awoke in a bed of crisp white sheets that felt warm from the heat of the bright autumn sun streaming through the French doors at the end of the bed, and from the body of her consort, Sean. The man sleeping next to her was a middle-aged, divorced, and quite successful stock broker in the city. She knew their cause needed money, and if she was to be queen, she needed a consort who could fund it. He owned a home in the south of France, which would also prove useful as a continental base. As her loyal soldier, Gus, was fluent in French, albeit Quebecois French, he would be the advance guard on the continent when that expansion began.

The shock of truth Sean experienced at the beginning had transformed into a new lease on life. He now viewed himself as a predator, and the world for his taking. Quite right too. In the time that he and Geraldine had been together, his personal income had doubled. As a thank you, he purchased an estate in the remote Highlands of Scotland for he and Geraldine to run together with the moon as God intended. A personal sanctuary only he and the Queen of Wolves were allowed to escape to.

Buck was the general of the army Geraldine was building. Without him, her prime order would never be fulfilled. That order was to procreate. London was the drainpipe of an old empire that still drew every nationality of human to it. It had become not just the world's financial capital, but a city-state wielding power most countries only dreamed of. Geraldine's subjects would infect the visitors from distant lands, who would then carry the disease back with them to their own countries.

After the infection, the new wolf was shepherded through their transformation on the heath. Thanks to Buck, it was a tightly controlled operation. Geraldine's reign would be a hundred years, regardless of how long she lived. In that time, the new wolves would be carefully chosen. Upper middle class, well-educated and well-traveled. The future establishment. In one hundred years, when the entire world was run by werewolves, then the next queen would decide her move from a position of power never before known by wolf kind.

Buck thought of his son, Trey. Somewhere in the middle of North America with Geraldine's daughter by his side. Calgary maybe? Was he following in Buck's and his sister's footsteps and going into law enforcement? Did they have a child yet? It's true he was not Trey's blood father. But, he liked to think he had a granddaughter or grandson out there. That his family was continuing. That the love he had given his son would be passed on. It gave Buck some solace. He knew he would likely never see Trey again.

Though Wikipedia and search engines have not solved the mystery of who was Jack the Ripper, they sure answered a lot of questions for Darkly. She learned that Cassandra attended St. Agnes the Blessed School for Girls in Shropshire from the age of eleven until seventeen. During her gap year, that year between the end of childhood's formal education and the beginning of university, she spent a year traveling with the son of the UK Ambassador to the United States. They began in Cape Town, and made their way to Sydney, and then Christchurch. After the Antipodean tour, they each entered the London School of Economics together, where their relationship continued.

Oliver Edward Samuel Rathscowl did not need Cassandra's family money. His was an old merchant family who survived comfortably the end of the aristocratic supremacy. He had even decided to marry Cassandra, once he was finished with his degree and placed in a diplomatic post. But, then, Cassandra's world was blown apart by a bullet to her father's head.

The great man had been discovered in bed with his housekeeper's teenage son, whom he had been paying handsomely for sexual favors. Unable to live with the scandal, he ended his life, creating a whole new scandal. It was all too much for a young man who saw marriage as a useful tool in navigating one's career, and he called it off with Cassandra. Six months later, he was married to Cassandra's best female friend, Bunny. Her only female friend. As the tabloids reported her comment to a gossip prone friend, she felt *emotionally raped by a stranger who should have been the foundation of her life and then raped again by the two people who had replaced family, yet turned out to be nothing more than strangers.*

Darkly delved deeper into the life of Oliver Rathscowl. Several consul generals under his belt, now an undersecretary position at the Foreign and Commonwealth Office, and two daughters, twins, about to turn eighteen. Tomorrow night. Was this the private party, wondered Darkly? A coming of age party? Was this the moment Cassandra could finally capitalize on to take her revenge? Were the betrayals decades before the reasons behind the woman who has it all choosing a life on all fours? Darkly would bet her life on it that it was.

A quick email to Vincetti secured an address for Oliver and wife Bunny. The Victorian detached house in Highgate was neighbors to the famous neo-gothic Victorian cemetery of the same name. Tall iron gates blocked access to a circular driveway in front of the rather austere brick home. The gates were open today, as delivery vans were unloading folding tables and chairs and tentpoles. The equipment was carried down the side of the house to what Darkly was certain was a larger than normal, for England, back garden. She walked right past the vans and up to the front door and placed her hand on the large brass knocker, striking it twice. She had a plan.

Within a few seconds, an attractive woman fast approaching fifty answered the door with a pleasant smile. Bunny, no doubt.

"Yes?"

"Oh, hello," replied Darkly. "My name is Lucy Hiller. I was taking a tour of your beautiful cemetery. I'm an American tourist, you see. Actually, I'm in London to sign a number of up-and-coming bands to my agency in New York. We're branching out across the pond. Anyway, I couldn't help but notice you're throwing a party, and I wondered if I might be able to interest you in one of my new clients?"

"Right. Well, that sounds lovely. But, I'm afraid my husband and I have already booked a band for our daughters' birthdays tomorrow night."

"Well, you can't blame a girl for trying. Can I ask what the name of the band is?"

"Of course. Just a minute," Bunny said without any sense of being put out.

Bunny walked to an exquisite desk in the entranceway and picked up a leather-bound diary and returned to the door.

"Moonkill," Bunny read from the diary. "Dreadful name, don't you think? An old friend of my husband's and mine is now managing the band. We reconnected after many years and agreed to hire the band as a favor to her more than anything. Oh, I do hope they're decent."

With that, Darkly said her goodbyes and made her way to the nearest tube station. She did not have reason to suspect she was being followed. But, Highgate Cemetery was a favorite stop for the more affluent and educated tourist, and so it was one of the spots that Gus spent time looking for the right candidates. The last person he expected to see among the tombstones was his old Mountie buddy, Darkly.

CHAPTER SEVENTEEN

"You'll arrest her, sheriff," said Geraldine, betraying a hint of pleasure.

"And then?" asked Buck.

"I'm queen," Geraldine asserted.

"I know. I was there."

Geraldine took one final drag on her cigarette and tossed it over the edge of the Cow. The wind blew Buck's hair, which was almost as long as Geraldine's now. He and Geraldine had adapted their appearances to the fashions of the outside world to not unpleasant effect. The sun was almost gone, but the bright lines cut into the rock below Buck's feet still gleamed bright. *Teddy was here. 1979.* Below the Cow outcrop, was the much smaller Calf boulder. The queen's sheriff looked behind him out over Ilkley Moor.

"Half an hour by train from a major metropolitan city, with almost 700 square miles of Yorkshire dales to run. We're taking too many chances in London, Geraldine."

"Fine," she agreed. "But, I'm serious about Darkly. Whatever she's doing in London, it ends tomorrow night. She's hunting us, Buck. She's chosen sides. You'll kill her if you have to."

Geraldine walked past Buck to a waiting Land Rover. Buck peered over the edge of the outcrop and watched Geraldine's glowing red cigarette butt burn itself out.

Darkly could look like anyone. Unusual for a beautiful girl. Beautiful by anyone's standards. But, do her hair up in a bun, apply a little too much eye make-up, wrap a black bow tie around her neck, and she transforms into a cater-waiter who is desperate to be noticed, and would thus be met with glances downward by guests eager not to engage the help. She was confident she could serve Bunny Rathscowl a canape and not be recognized as the talent manager from the day before.

Darkly walked right through the gates of the Highgate home, up to the caterer's utility van and picked up a blue rack of trayed sandwiches. She followed the other waiters down the side of the house to the back garden, which was covered in a white tent and lit by chandeliers.

In the center of the tent, was a rectangular koi pond. Rose bushes lined the edges of the tent, and at the rear of the structure, a one-foot platform backed up to a hedgerow. At the other end, were French doors that led into the kitchen. Darkly walked through and placed the rack of sandwiches on the center island. She turned to go, and was stopped by a loud, brash voice.

"Oi. I am absolutely fucking certain I told you in particular that nothing, I mean nothing, is to be left on kitchen surfaces. I'm going to have to sanitize that all over again."

The wiry chef glared at Darkly. He had that nervous energy about him that indicated to Darkly he would need to pop into the loo shortly to feed his coke habit.

"Do I need to send you home?" asked the chef.

"No, chef," Darkly replied and picked up the rack.

"The walk-in's that way," said the chef, pointing to a short corridor beyond a breakfast nook.

Darkly carried the rack past a pantry and into a walk-in refrigerator, whose door was wide open. Two girls with tightly bound buns of dark hair were opening boxes of champagne and cold drinks, separating itcms out for a kids and an adult bar. Darkly placed the rack on top of the stack of blue racks already in the refrigerator.

After several trips back and forth from the front drive, Darkly had built another stack of blue racks. With the last rack in place, Darkly walked down the short corridor to find something else to keep herself busy while waiting for the party to begin. As she was about to emerge into the kitchen, she heard a voice she had been anticipating.

"Bunny! So good to see you."

Darkly slipped into the pantry at the sound of the two women kissing each other on each cheek and walked right into the chef, holding cans of condensed milk. He opened his mouth to yell, and Darkly closed it with her own mouth. She began kissing him, parting his mouth with her tongue, while she reached down to feel around under his apron. He smelled of grease, garlic and cigarettes, but Darkly was a fine actress.

"Don't drop the cans," she ordered, and the chef kissed her back, while Darkly listened to the conversation in the kitchen. Then the pain set in. The chef's tongue felt like sandpaper against her own. Then her mouth felt like she had just chugged a jar of sriracha. She was kissing a killer.

"Olly's keeping the girls occupied in town. It's not a surprise, but we want them to be amazed when they arrive."

"It's going to be a night they won't forget, Bunny. I promise. My band has just arrived. I'm going to help them get situated."

"I'll have the chef whip something up for them before they play, Cassandra."

"Not necessary. They already have plans to eat later tonight."

Darkly listened to Cassandra walk out the French doors, and then broke off the kiss with the chef, taking a deep intake of breath and relief.

"I have that effect," the chef gloated. "Let's take up where we left off at the end of the party."

The chef would be off her case for the rest of the night. She left him standing in the pantry still holding two cans of condensed milk and a doe-eyed expression on his face. She walked past Bunny, who was checking things off on a list. The two women smiled at each other, and the lady of the house, as Darky suspected, didn't see anyone in Darkly's face she had met before.

Darkly stepped up to the glass of the French doors and watched as Cassandra placed her hand on Toma's shoulder. He brushed it away and stormed off. When Cassandra turned her back to the house, Darkly slipped out and followed Toma out of the tent.

Toma turned to look for who was following him, but Darkly had already pushed her way between two holy bushes, stifling the hundred pricks of pain brought about by the crowned plant. He pulled a pack of Dunhill cigarettes from his jacket pocket and lit one.

"The great thing about being a wolf. The lungs heal themselves. We're almost invincible. Gods, really. Well, demi-gods."

Toma looked behind him to see Cassandra approaching.

"Wolves don't seek revenge. They hunt for survival," Toma countered.

Darkly was putting her calf muscles to good use, holding her crouch in complete silence.

"Did you ever hear the story about the Russian trapper? He brought down a male wolf that was stalking his mink traps. The wolf's mate came for him. Followed him miles back to his cabin in the middle of bum-fuck Siberia. Killed him in the outhouse while he was going number two. They know this because the hunter that found his frozen body described it as covered in shite."

"This has nothing to do with me," insisted Toma.

"No? You don't like the money? You don't like playing your al-right-at-best music in front of important people?"

Toma bristled at that, and Cassandra took his hand.

"Listen to me. You do have the potential to be an amazing talent. With my unwavering support. I just need you to show me your support. Come on, it's not like we're going to kill them. You're going to give the girls a gift. A gift that will just happen to devastate their parents."

Toma stepped away from Cassandra.

"Or get a real job."

With that, Cassandra walked away. Toma begrudgingly followed, like a puppy with its tail between its legs, and Darkly had an idea of what the night held for two young women. The writhing.

Zoe and India entered the tent to the roar of their friends and beaming parents. Cassandra stood by them. The two people she had been closest to in her life. The man and woman who had been her family, when her own family was nothing more than a chequebook. The two people who betrayed her. She had no family.

As Darkly glided through the crowd with trays of champagne and hors d'oeuvres, she watched Toma and his bad boy bass player seduce the two birthday girls. They serenaded them, rocked their world. Darkly knew there was something more hormonal and primal taking place. The writhing was the wolf word that described the sexual magnetism werewolves inflicted on non-weres. With the right ambience, the chances of *no* were nil. Introduce a guitar into the mix, and a hundred guests become the ghosts of peripheral vision.

So it was with the two birthday girls. They had eyes only for Toma and his bass player. Their giggles and bouncing evolved into a comatose swaying. Ignored, their friends drifted away into other groups. The golden calves were separated from the herd. Cassandra caught Toma's eye and gave him a nod.

"Thank you very much. We're going to take a little dinner break, and we'll be back," Toma announced to a round of applause.

Toma finished the set and stepped off the stage. He whispered something in Zoe's ear, who grabbed her sister's hand and walked back to the house. Toma nodded at his bass player. They ordered a drink at the bar and accepted a few compliments before walking into the house themselves.

Darkly observed the whole maneuver and knew exactly what to do. She tattled. She walked right up to Oliver Rathscowl and asked him for a word. His embarrassment at being pulled aside by staff was quickly forgotten.

"Sir," explained Darkly, "I believe your daughters have taken a couple of the boys in the band up to their rooms."

"Uh. Alright."

Oliver seemed unsure of what to do.

"They aren't going upstairs to talk, sir," Darkly continued. "I overheard one of your daughters telling the other that she was looking forward to losing her virginity tonight."

Oliver's face went pale.

"Thank you."

Darkly nodded, and Oliver rushed off to grab his wife. He pulled her away from a conversation to whisper in her ear, and after the same widening of eyes, the two rushed into the house.

Cassandra noticed the alarm on the parents' faces and looked in Darkly's direction, finally seeing the waitress for who she was. Darkly beat Cassandra into the house. Both women ran past the confused chef for the front of the home and up the staircase to the second story, where they arrived in time to see both sisters, only wearing panties, thrown out of a bedroom. The bass player followed them out and bolted down the staircase. Darkly let him go. He wasn't who she was after tonight.

"How dare you! In my home, no less."

Oliver was laying into Toma, and Bunny slapped both of her daughters across their faces, not knowing what else she should do in such a situation.

"Olly!" Cassandra screamed at the top of her lungs. The girls stopped crying, and Oliver and a naked Toma stepped out of the room slowly.

"Yes, Cassandra?" Oliver asked, subdued by the scream.

"You ripped me in two."

"Excuse me?"

"Both of you," Cassandra said in Bunny's direction. "You were my only family, and you cut out my heart and left nothing in its place. These girls could have been mine. Ours, Olly."

Bunny moved to put herself between her daughters and Cassandra.

"Well, they're not. Get out of my house, and take him with you."

Bunny pointed at Toma, doing her best not to look lower than the waist. Cassandra just replied with a light-hearted chuckle.

"Oh, Bunny. I've been saving myself for your family. My first kill."

And that was the last thing Cassandra said. She walked up to Oliver and grabbed his face. She planted a hard kiss on his lips, which he pulled back from to stare into eyes that were becoming swirling pools of yellow ink.

Darkly reached for the gun under her belt. There was nothing there. Cassandra glanced at Darkly and held up the gun she had successfully lifted off a Mountie. She removed the clip from the gun and threw it down the stairwell, then dropped the gun on the floor.

"Shit," said Darkly.

"What's wrong with your eyes, Cassandra?" asked Oliver, stepping backwards into the naked Toma.

Cassandra smiled through a mouth that was narrowing, pushing the teeth forward. Her head then fell forward, as loud cracks accompanied the buckling of her back and the emergence of a hump. Cassandra threw her head back and half howled, half screamed, then fell forward on all fours, knocking Oliver back onto Toma. Both men toppled to the floor like dominoes, and Cassandra's growing claws landed on Oliver's chest, digging into his flesh.

Bunny screamed, as Cassandra opened her mouth to bite off Oliver's face. At the last minute, before a face became a gaping, bloody crater, a shot rang out. The bullet entered Cassandra's skull and partially exited her forehead. The tip of the silver bullet looked back at Oliver like a third eye.

Darkly turned slowly to look behind her. All the eyes on the landing followed hers. There, standing at the top of the staircase, was Buck, Geraldine and Gus. It was Buck who had fired the shot.

"All she had to do was kill you, Darkly. That was her only job. Revenge is a poor reason to hunt. We hunt for love. Shall we take this outside?" asked Geraldine rhetorically.

Darkly nodded, and Buck waved his gun at Toma, who then joined Darkly.

"Give him your coat," Buck said to Gus.

Gus removed his coat and handed it to Toma, who covered himself. Gus ushered Darkly and Toma down the stairs.

"Mr. and Mrs. Rathscowl, I suggest you forget what happened here tonight. Or I will come for your daughters."

Zoe and India grabbed hold of their mother.

"We understand," Bunny agreed and glared at Oliver, who was still in shock.

"Ah, yes. Quite."

"Good."

And with that, Buck lifted Cassandra off Oliver and threw her body over his shoulder like a sack of flower. Geraldine descended the stairs first, followed by Toma, then Darkly, then Gus and Buck.

"I'm sorry, Darkly," whispered Gus. "A lot's changed in a year. Geraldine's more than family now."

The group left the house, where a Land Rover waited in the circular drive. Buck threw Cassandra's body in the back and opened

the front-passenger door for Geraldine. Gus opened the back-pas-
senger side door for Darkly and Toma.

"Oi."

Darkly turned to see the chef standing in the doorway to the
home.

"Leaving without saying goodbye? How 'bout your number
then, love?"

The chef picked his fingernails with a large knife.

"We don't want any trouble," warned Buck.

"Could have fooled me. Murder is sort of the definition of trouble, isn't it?"

At that point, two waiters appeared from both sides of the
house, each with guns pointed at the Land Rover.

"The undersecretary is a target of extremists. It's my job to protect him. Let the girl go. I'm afraid it wouldn't have worked for us,
darling. I'm married. Be on your way."

Buck raised his hands in the air and shook his head at Darkly.
She grabbed Toma's hand and ran.

"Take them into custody," the chef commanded his waiters.

"Belay that order."

Oliver Rathscowl stepped onto the front landing.

"Sir?" asked the chef, incredulous.

"Let them go," confirmed Oliver.

"Sir."

The chef nodded at his waiters, who lowered their weapons.
Buck and Gus got into the Land Rover, and it pulled into the street.

"Let's get back to the party, Nigel."

"Yes, sir," the chef replied dutifully but put-out.

Oliver and his bodyguards returned to the guests.

CHAPTER EIGHTEEN

Darkly and Toma climbed the cast iron gates and dropped down into Highgate Cemetery. Darkly gave Toma the universal silence symbol, with a finger to her mouth. They ran down one of the lanes of homes of the dead, ducking behind the last brick tomb in the short row, and listened.

They heard a car motor near the front gates cut off. Darkly grabbed Toma's hand and pulled him into the trees behind the tomb.

"They know we're here. There's nowhere else to hide," Darkly whispered while making her way forward. "They know we couldn't stick to the road. We need to make it over the wall into the public park. That's where we'll be most vulnerable. The park exits at the top of the hill that leads down to the tube station. It's a bit of a hike, but if we're lucky, there'll be a passing taxi."

Darkly and Toma continued their meandering route through gravestones. At the statue of a Victorian woman in repose atop her own grave, they heard the first howl. The wolves were in the cemetery. Their odds of making it out were now greatly diminished.

Their scent would lead Buck, Gus and Geraldine straight to them. Angry, not quite themselves, and hungry.

Darkly broke through the last tangle of raspberry bushes and vines and looked up at a brick wall too tall to scale.

"Feel for holes in the brick," she ordered Toma, not bothering to whisper.

The noise of twigs breaking continuously behind them indicated that the wolves had their scent.

"Hurry," she added.

Darkly and Toma moved quickly along the wall, feeling for bricks that were missing or jutting out from the wall due to settling of the wall's foundation.

"Here," said Darkly excitedly. "Help me up."

Toma offered Darkly a lift, and she stepped onto a jagged piece of brick above the head of a crumbling angel, where the wall had cracked and begun to separate. She pressed her fingertips into the grooves between the brick and climbed to the top of the wall. Toma hopped up beneath her, as she flung a leg over the cap of the wall. The growling was now only twenty yards away. The wolves were following the path the two escapees took along the base of the wall.

Darkly reached down and offered her hand, pulling Toma up to join her, as a pair of jaws lunged at the air just below their feet, taking them by complete surprise. One of the wolves was more silent and closer than they thought. Buck. Darkly and Toma practically fell into Waterlow Park and were up running across a field, uphill, a second later. They flew across a bridge over a duck pond and continued up a paved pathway toward the exit of the park. Toma looked behind him.

"Don't look back," Darkly chastised, but did the same.

Three wolves were halfway across the field that bordered the cemetery wall.

"Fuck," shouted Darkly at the heavens. "They found a way out."

The two reached the exit, as the wolves reached the bridge, and scaled the much more manageable gate designed merely to let the neighborhood know the park was closed, rather than to deter grave robbers. The Mountie and the rocker were now doing their best to run down Highgate Hill without falling. The high- street shops were in sight. Darkly looked across the road, where a taxi was letting off an inebriated passenger.

"There!" she yelled and pointed at the same time.

They darted across the road and dove into the back of the black cab, startling the driver.

"Drive!" yelled Toma.

"Hold on a goddamn minute. This is my cab, and I have the right to refuse service."

"Shut up," Darkly interrupted, "and look in your rearview mirror."

The driver did as he was instructed and saw three large wolves barreling down on his vehicle. In this case, the fact that objects may appear closer than they are, didn't cause any hesitation. He rammed the gear shift into drive and shot off.

"Mother Mary of God," he exclaimed.

Behind the cab, the drunk opening his front door merely shrugged, as he watched the three beasts run past his home.

The driver sailed through a red light, just avoided a collision with another vehicle and drove the wrong way down a one-way before turning onto Junction Road. A mile later, everyone took a breath.

"I think they're gone," Darkly broke the silence. "Cheshire Hotel, Paddington, please. Then I'll need you to make a run to Heathrow."

"Yes ma'am," the driver stuttered.

At the hotel, Darkly pulled out a drawer to a vanity, flipped it over and tore off an envelope of cash taped to the bottom.

"This will be their next stop," Darkly said, handing Toma the envelope. This is two thousand pounds. You need to get back in the cab and get on the next flight out of Heathrow to Seattle."

Darkly looked around her for a pen. She picked one off the floor and grabbed Toma's hand, writing a number on his palm.

"When you land, go to a payphone and call this number, collect. The man who answers will come get you and take you to Marielle and your son. Don't leave them again."

Toma nodded. Darkly could see in his eyes that once he got where he was going, he was staying put. Good.

"And drop the *a*, Tom. *Go!*"

Tom paused at the door long enough to thank Darkly, and then she watched him from her room's window get into the cab and drive away. Darkly then threw a few personal items into a bag, and left the hotel via the back entrance. She walked down a short flight of steps, took a step into the alley and turned in a circle. What was she doing? Where was she going? She walked to the brick wall and leaned her hands and forehead against it. She took two deep breaths to collect herself.

"You look like you could use a drink."

Darkly looked around for the voice. Across the narrow alleyway was a young man in a sleeping bag.

"You're right," she replied. "Helluva night."

"Bet it doesn't beat my night," he said with a big grin.

Darkly walked over to him.

"I don't suppose you know where a Canadian girl can find a taste of home?"

"Canadian, huh? Maybe I do. There's a place on Maiden Lane, Covent Garden. The Maple Leaf."

Darkly reached into her bag and pulled out a fifty pound note. She handed it to the man.

"Whoa. That's fifty pounds."

"Thanks for the tip."

And with that, Darkly, knew where she was going next.

Darkly got off the lift at Covent Garden tube station and glanced at the large color map on the wall. Maiden Lane was a short stroll through the old market, now renovated posh tourist shops. She could see The Strand below where she stood, and the crowds of theatre-goers returning home. She turned onto Maiden Lane before reaching the hustle and bustle and was greeted by a red neon maple leaf.

There were a few memories of home inside, like the stuffed moose head and a pair of tattered mukluks nailed to the wall. Darkly was pleased to see meatloaf and mashed potatoes on the menu. She sat at the bar and ordered a pint of her favorite lager from home.

She was finishing off the plate of comfort food and about to order a second pint, when she felt the arm brush against her back. She had faced the windows and entrance out of habit and turned to consider Buck's face. He was seated on the stool next to hers. He was good. She never saw him come in.

"Can I get your second?" Buck asked, pointing at the near empty pint glass.

"I'd like that."

The bartender appeared in front of Buck.

"Two of what she's drinking, please."

The bartender nodded and delivered two cold pints to two people who had earned their thirst in ways he could not imagine.

"Did you beat it out of the homeless guy?"

Darkly spit the words into her plate.

"We're not monsters, Darkly. I paid him."

"I gave him fifty quid."

"That's mean of you, Darkly. I gave him one hundred."

At that, Darkly lightened up a bit.

"So you really thought you'd be rid of me for good by now?"

"Sicking Cassandra on you was Geraldine's idea. I knew nothing about it. Even if I had known, I wouldn't have been too worried. I don't believe there is any situation you can't handle, constable."

Buck looked at a booth in a corner of the pub. Darkly followed his eyes to see Geraldine, Gus, and two new members of the werewolf species staring back at her.

"Things have become rather political since moving to London, Darkly."

"I can see that, Buck."

"We've revived some old traditions. It made sense at the time."

"And now?"

"Now?" Buck mused. "Now, I long for simpler times."

"I think you've adjusted to big city life just fine, sheriff."

"We're an adaptable species. It's part of our success. And, make no mistake, Darkly. No one, not even you, can stop our success. We've set things in motion that will bring this whole world much desired peace in the long run."

Darkly took a drink and shook her head.

"I've heard it all before in the interrogation room. Oh, I believe *you* believe the end justifies the means."

"Darkly, I've told some lies about you. It wasn't to keep my people safe from you. It was to keep you safe from us. I'm giving you one last chance. Go back home. Lead a long life fighting drug trafficking and money laundering. A normal, happy life."

"And look the other way when it comes to you?"

Darkly polished off her second pint.

"And what if I decide I'm partial to London weather and want to hang around a bit? You got anymore silver bullets in your gun?"

"I owe you. But Geraldine will keep trying until she succeeds."

Darkly raised her empty glass to Geraldine. One of the queen's new men raised his glass to her and received a sharp reprimand from Geraldine.

"Oh, they're bright recruits, Buck. I think I'll take my chances."

Darkly leant in and kissed Buck tenderly on the lips. When she pulled away, she had his wallet in her hands. She opened it, and removed forty pounds for the bartender. She handed Buck back his wallet and slipped off her stool. At the door, she saw Geraldine's group get up to follow her out. Buck beat them to her.

The second they got outside, Buck grabbed Darkly's arm and spoke quickly, with no sense of humor carried forward from the intimate exchange at the bar.

"Run, Darkly Stewart. Run for the river. It's your only chance. They won't be able to follow your scent in the water. Meet me in Romania. One week."

It was Buck's turn to kiss Darkly. He grabbed her neck and made a brief meal of her lips.

"Run," he whispered.

Darkly ran, and Buck turned to grab the royal goon exiting the front door. He grabbed him by the coat and ran his head through the door's pane of glass like a battering ram.

Gus took his protective place in front of Geraldine, letting the second goon attack Buck. Buck punched the large man in the stomach, which achieved nothing. The man picked Buck up and threw him into the middle of the road. Buck removed his gun, and the man kicked it out of his hand.

"Enough!"

The word was loud enough to stop Darkly, too, who turned to look back and see Geraldine step forward into the empty lane. It was late. The theatre-goers were in cabs, returning to the suburbs. She picked up Buck's gun. She turned away from Darkly and spoke closely with Gus. She then turned back to face Darkly, lowered the gun, and shot Buck in the chest.

Darkly opened her mouth to scream, but no sound came out. Geraldine said something to the two goons, but Darkly did not stick around to learn what that was. She ran full sprint for the

Thames. Her heart was beating faster than it had ever beat before. Grief mixed with adrenaline, as she turned onto The Strand. Behind her, she heard Geraldine, Gus and the others raise their voices in unison to howl over Buck's body.

Darkly bolted past the iconic Savoy Hotel and took a quick glance behind her as she ran across the road and turned onto the dual-carriageway that led to Waterloo Bridge. Two wolves were turning onto The Strand, growling and snapping at the air, forcing two horrified late diners to turn and pound on the just locked door of Simpson's-in-the-Strand, begging to be let back in.

The Mountie made it to the middle of Waterloo Bridge. No one else was crossing and able to bear witness to what happened next. The Thames is a tidal river, and it was high tide as Darkly climbed up onto the railing, balancing perfectly over the fast-drifting water below her. The two wolves chasing her slowed their pace dramatically when they hit the bridge. A black shrieking shadow suddenly swooped down from the sky and pecked at the wolves' eyes. A guardian raven. But, Darkly's attackers could only be delayed. They had her scent and would not stop before plunging their fangs into her neck. She couldn't outrun them further. There was no choice before her but to dive into the river below, where she would surely drown. This was the end of the road for both wolf and woman.

Darkly calmed herself. Her life moved at the speed of light, every second of it, every beautiful and sad moment projected in her mind like a movie, when she stepped off the railing. Her childhood. Laughing with her mother, watching her mother die. Being swooped up into her adoptive father's arms on the side of the highway. Telling her adoptive mother that she hated her, then clinging to her waist for forgiveness. Then her life as a Mountie, the death of her partner, the thrill of Buck's glancing touch. Then the bullet to Buck's heart and the sound of her own heartbeat louder than she had heard it in her ears since the womb.

Darkly hit the water and sank. Shock gave way to panic. Panic to despair, and the woman who tasted death surrendered to her own doom in the form of a rip current that would carry her out into the Thames Estuary, the sea, and then oblivion.

CHAPTER NINETEEN

Darkly looked up at the Milky Way stretched across the sky. She felt the coolness of the black water against her body. It was not as cold as it should have been, she thought. She must be numb, but she was treading water. Sleep swimming? Was that a thing? The lights of London were growing smaller and smaller up river. How long had she been in the water? How had she survived?

The current was moving quickly, and a foreboding structure was rushing to meet her. A ship? Darkly reached out to touch it. It was concrete. There was a building in the middle of the river! If she didn't act immediately, the building would be behind her in seconds. She kicked out her legs and threw her arms up the side of the structure, desperately searching blindly for something to grab hold of. Thankfully, the concrete was rough and weathered with imperfections.

Darkly dug her nails into the pockmarks in the cement and held on. Stationary, she felt just how strong the undertow was. It carried her feet farther down river, until she climbed out of the water. She pulled herself up to a railing and slinked underneath it onto a platform. Her body was awfully lithe for being submerged in cold water, she thought. She should be stiff as a board. Darkly looked out at a row of what looked like small aircraft hangers that stretched the width of The Thames. This must be the famed Thames Barrier, that prevented London's center being periodically drowned by the North Sea.

There was a dim light above a door that must lead to the interior of the structure. Darkly walked under the light and leapt back as though she had stepped on hot coals. What had she just seen? With mixed trepidation and elation, Darkly slid her foot forward again under the light.

Buck had told Darkly she was special, that her bloodline was ancient. The rules that applied to other wolves may not apply to her. She may be cured of the curse, or she may not be. She closed her eyes tightly, took a seat under the lightbulb and reopened her eyes to peer down at a pool of collected rain water. A wolf looked back at her. Jet black fur and eyes of steel gray. She placed her paw in the middle of the reflection and looked up at the moon in the sky.

Darkly understood in that moment just how special she was. There was no clouding of her mind. She was perfectly lucid. The primitive and intuitive had not supplanted the rational. She knew exactly who and what she was. She was Darkly Stewart...Mountie... and Werewolf. Darkly, the werewolf, threw back her head and howled for all that was lost to her and now found.

EPILOGUE

B ecoming queen was not something Eluned had looked forward to. Beyond the duty and weight of decision-making, she was the sacrificial lamb, embodying all the terrible consequences of her decisions for generations to come. Half a century from now, wolves would be cursing her name and defiling her grave, if history was anything to go by.

But, the alphas had gathered. Like a conclave of cardinals, they had gathered and prayed. And Eluned was who God revealed to the majority. If she did not accept her divine responsibility, she would be required to give up her life to make way for another. Regardless, every queen becomes queen the way every alpha becomes alpha. Power most be usurped. With an alpha, exile had become the more civilized sentence on the defeated. But, for a new queen, an alpha must die, and Eluned assume the emptied authority ordinarily occupied by a man.

So, on the eve after she accepted the silver mail, Eluned stood above the young Alpha of Edinburgh, the point of a silver sword hovering over his heart. He was a young man, not yet thirty. Two children and a wife. They would be exalted above all but Eluned. The young alpha faced his death with courage because of this knowledge.

Eluned ran him through, and the conclave howled in unison.

Next book in THE DARKLY STEWART MYSTERIES…

RAVEN IN A WOLF'S WOOD

To the lawless forests of the near east, where the legends of Europe's monsters were born, Darkly escapes…in search of allies. Romania is a place where shapeshifters take flight, and where Darkly uncovers a remnant of her family line.

THE AUTHOR

DG Wood lives in Los Angeles with his wife, Wendy, daughter, Audrey, and little werewolf, Simon. He is currently hard at work on adapting The Darkly Stewart Series for television. When not writing or working in film and television production, Wood gives talks on the art of enjoying whisky. He is a graduate of the London Academy of Music and Dramatic Art and a voting member of the British Academy of Film & Television Arts.

Printed in Great
Britain
by Amazon